The Principle
of
Camouflage

FRANCES BINGHAM

TWO RAVENS
PRESS

Published by Two Ravens Press Ltd.
Taigh nam Fitheach
26 Breanish, Uig
Isle of Lewis HS2 9HB
United Kingdom

www.tworavenspress.com

The right of Frances Bingham to be identified as author of
this work has been asserted by her in accordance with the
Copyright, Designs and Patent Act, 1988.
© Frances Bingham, 2011.

ISBN: 978-1-906120-56-6

British Library Cataloguing in Publication Data: a CIP record
for this book can be obtained from the British Library.

Designed and typeset in Sabon by Two Ravens Press;
cover design by Two Ravens Press.

Cover art: *Sea light* by Liz Mathews (www.pottersyard.co.uk)

Printed in Poland on Forest Stewardship
Council-accredited paper.

About the Author

Frances Bingham has published fiction, non-fiction and poetry, most recently *Journey from Winter* (Carcanet, 2008) the biographical critical edition of Valentine Ackland's poems. Frances has performed at literary festivals, read poetry live on *Woman's Hour*, and contributed to the Radio 4 series *From the Ban to the Booker*. She is the daughter of the Scots historian and biographer Caroline Bingham, and now lives and works in London with her partner Liz Mathews.

For more information about the author, see
www.tworavenspress.com

Acknowledgements

I'm grateful to The Society of Authors, as the Literary Representative of the Estate of Virginia Woolf, for permission to quote from *Between the Acts*.

My thanks also to all the friends and colleagues who have asked about the book for their support and interest. I'd like to record that Muriel Worsdell and Caroline Bingham both gave me infinite help and encouragement in many continuing ways. And as always, more than thanks to Liz Mathews, my first reader and best inspirer.

For Liz Mathews

I

Kezia

Here is the picture. It is a painting. Hesketh always painted on wood, and the colours in the picture are the colours of pale scoured driftwood – salt-silvered beach detritus, white stones churned smooth by the sea's incessant cobbling, bleached trees. Even the sky is opaque like a dull pearl – the seawater gunmetal grey scummed with bottleglass green. It takes a moment to notice the figure in the landscape standing there, back to the sea, gazing at the unseen inland where we observing sit. A young airman perhaps – the ghost of a pilot hovering on the beach where he came to shore – some scarred hero regretting a botched sacrifice. The figure, alone in that great space – head flung back, body leaning on a stick with crippled swagger – expresses an absurd bravado. It is very recognisably Fitz – cigarette in hand, greatcoat draped cape-like over shoulders, arm in the silk scarf sling which makes a kingfisher-blue flash over the heart.

Was Hesketh laughing at Fitz – is the portrait a parody? I think not – the answer is there in the face – so tenderly painted that each brush stroke is a caress which acknowledges heroism rather than mocks it. There is some irony there – certainly – but not (I think) at the subject's expense. Perhaps at mine? When Hesketh gave me the painting she said it should be entitled *Some day my prince will come*. I did not understand her, then. But now I know that Hesketh did try to produce – someone – suitable. She got more than she bargained for.

1

Oh, what could be worse than being a princess – condemned always to wait, never herself to act, but to be rescued, awoken, disenchanted, given as the reward thrown in free with half the kingdom. There's no escape from that destiny – no spell to break that enchantment – I know. If a powerful parent – Hesketh, say – makes her daughter a princess, surely the least to be done for the child is to provide an appropriate prince when the time is right. No? (I don't think so either.) Otherwise, the unfortunate young woman may be eaten by a sea-monster – or perhaps condemned to marry one. But first, there must be some situation to be rescued from – a dragon demanding maiden sacrifice – an accursed sleep – wicked stepsisters – mistaken identity as a shepherdess. All I had was my isolated state – from which I had no wish to be saved.

Our exile was determined by Hesketh – but I can't imagine that she intended us to stay in that remote place for so long – ten years islanded on our own – transforming me from robust child to mateless sea-spoused half-woman. Her escape was supposed only to be a temporary flight followed by a restoration. Even as a child sleeping on Hesketh's knee in the train while she wept all night, I knew that my father had not sent us away – only made it impossible for her to stay. Perhaps she imagined that he would follow us – realise his true wishes – reverse his degradation – change everything. Of course that was not what he would allow to happen. Treachery – the worst of sins – might be pardoned by a person as magnanimous as my mother (I thought), but I did not hope. She would have had much to forgive – not least that journey – the kindness of friends who know what unspeakable things are wrong – the inadequate sanctuary.

I remember – again – our night arrival at Saltstreet with no light, no food, no fire, only the noise of the sea inexplicably close. It was like a dank cave. We slept in our overcoats clutched together on the damp sofa and woke to cold – cold – monochrome. But I still see myself – half Hesketh's height – holding her hand against the wind, shrieking like the seabirds which wheeled above us as I saw where we were. The beach was there – wide – wet sand intricately overlaid with a lace-pattern of small shells and stones stretching as far as my long sight could see on either side of us and ahead to the curved horizon, where Hesketh said we could see the curvature of the earth. Behind us, the house stood in the dunes – not raised up on a cliff but on a low unstable promontory, merely a shingle finger extended into the sand. It had a low stone foundation which looked like a jumble of flints and sea-bricks, then clinkered and caulked wooden walls like an upturned boat above – all so roughly tumbled together the sea might have thrown it up there as a storm-drift. (I was delighted, despite my frozen face and aching voice.) At the seaward side there was a row of cantilevered glass windows escaping from the roof – which I perceived as a makeshift sideways-set lighthouse lantern.

'The studio,' said Hesketh half to herself. 'North light.' Then – almost violently – 'I shall work here.'

So as soon as the fires were lit – we had eaten – started to unpack – heat water – we went up to that long room, the sail loft, still the centre of my dreams. It was icy then – the whitened walls and pale grey lino floor seemed light with frost. The huge windows were filled with chill sea. We carried up the big boxes I thought of as magic, opened out into their ziggurats of little shelves and drawers. As Hesketh began to sort out her paint tubes and bottles the smell of home spread out – the easels, tall stools, canvas racks and work benches were intensely familiar to me already. I was content to know that Hesketh would make her alchemy here – while I could watch – witness it.

I chose one of the two mirror-image tiny bedrooms – the one with the blue bedspread not the red. Both faced onto the marsh. I woke in the night. The cold air on my face – the unfamiliar weight of the blanket-pile – puzzled me – I was afraid. Under the frantic drumming of all the shutters and windows rattling in their sockets was another noise – a continuous low drone like a giant bomber's threatening hum. I sat up in bed. Hesketh appeared in the doorway – a sudden apparition – carrying a dangerously-angled oil lamp. I stared round-eyed as the noise rose and fell around the house. She smiled at me, regal in her black and gold dragon robe.

'Be not afraid, the isle is full of noises, which give delight and hurt not,' she said, sitting down by my feet.

'It is practically an island, isn't it?'

'Certainly an island.'

'Will you call me Friday if I call you Crusoe?'

'Certainly, Friday.'

'What is that noise, Crusoe?'

'It's the sea playing its bagpipes. Now go back to sleep if you can.'

I heard her moving about, not in her bedroom but in the studio – later she always slept on the divan in there – close to her work. I listened to the sea's musical efforts. I think I knew already that I would never be able to hear other voices.

For the truth is – it wasn't Hesketh's fault that I lost my freedom – it wasn't Hesketh that I was bound to – it was this place. She brought me too young to somewhere too strong for me – I was in thrall to it – overwhelmed by the gods of the island – I dedicated myself to them so that I was unhappy outside the sacred precinct. I suppose – to put it another

4

way – my roots were torn up – I survived the upheaval – the transplantation – but could not face another. Yet – though that is surely part of it – there was something else – more profoundly true. Hesketh told me once that I was born in a caul – so that I'd never drown – the sea's mark of favour to a child already dedicated to its service.

This sea here – this grim grey uncompromising sea – claimed me. I have memories of another sea – a clear crystalline welcoming sea – which I loved – which I wept to leave. But this English sea runs in my veins – ungainsayable – it possessed me then – as it does now. I asked Hesketh if she'd kept the caul – no shadow crossed her face – she just laughed – said no, she'd given it to a sailor who couldn't swim, and was afraid of death by water. This answer satisfied me – like all the answers she gave – it was complete.

Crambo

This island's mine. It isn't an island but practically is one. I was here before they came, will be here after they've gone. My island runs from the little creek where the holy stream flows down from the low hill and across the marsh and cuts sand-cliffs through the higher-up beach and opens out like feather-grasses lower where it meets the shallows of the sea, all the way along the beach along along past the old boathouse, past the wreck, past the sand-dune islands in the bay and the giant whale wishbone beached up by the shingle cliff and my rocking stone to the pebble mountains where the great gravel-spit starts. Then the deepwater channel comes out, the inlet up to Saltstreet quay where the boats are, miles upstream. Don't go further than that, don't know anything past that. Inland, over the dunes and past the marsh to the church green as far as the lane, to the end of the ditch by the sea embankment wall, it's all mine. Beyond, I don't know. Seawards, outland, doesn't belong to anyone, not even Her. When the tide goes back sometimes and the underneath sand is out so far you can walk to the wreck and the seal-bank, I think it's mine. But the water always comes back.

My kingdom opens and closes, doubles and halves, twice most days. Sometimes the sea comes up over the dunes and covers the marsh, all water then except the tops of the sand-hills. When the tide comes in it brings me things, tribute, presents anyway. I keep all the glass. We burn the wood, if it's been in the sea for long it shrinks as it dries, a plank becomes a splinter. The dead things are like that too. Nails and rope and string and fishing-line and net, I make my things with, and cork floats and empty tins and bones and shells and dried creatures. I don't like feathers, I never touch them.

One time the sea was sunset colour at midday as it came in and the beach too when the sea reached it, and it was shoals of oranges, which are fruits, and as it went back from the whole tideline it left drifts of them on the shingle. Sometimes it's razorshells or sea urchins or weed left in neat crescents deeply banked, but these were oranges and the wood of their broken boxes. I ate them and ate them, salty and bitter, and I carried hundreds of them away to hide and bury, and up to Her and Kezia. They still liked me then, and they made sharp sweet jam out of them, but it was still distantly salty. The best time, I saw a thing in the water like a great grey-white jelly fish, big as a sail, spread out clinging like oil on the surface of the water. I got it, and it was all stitching and ropes on silken sodden material. They told me it was a parachute. All my shirts are made of it now. My trousers are a red Yarmouth sail which came up the creek. They'll never wear out.

In the summer, I mostly live in the dunes. There's water where the stream comes down, not salt or brackish, and the sweet spring on the other side of the marsh. All the animals go there. I eat fish, all the kinds I can catch, eels and crabs mostly, but you have to cook them. Raw, I eat whelks and urchins and cockles and oysters, always oysters. The others, mussels and clams and scallops, need cooking really. Birds aren't nice raw either, and because of the feathers I can't touch them, so I don't eat them. I like eggs though, when I can get them. Some seaweed is possible, when there isn't anything else I make soup with it, like drinking the sea. Samphire just tastes of sea-twigs too. There is a lovely time, when there are blackberries and little nuts in the hedges, and mushrooms, and wild apples and field leaves, but it doesn't last long. In the winter, there's only what comes out of the sea. Before they came, when I was smaller, this was my place, alone. Sometimes, rarely, I saw other people here, mostly the fishermen coming along on the off-chance, or digging for bait-worms. An old chap sent to mend the fence, postman curvetting on his bicycle, vicar in a car, I might see once in a while. Women came too, collecting shellfish in baskets, or eggs, and children from the village or inland folk came to get wood. Not often, though. In summer, visitors used to come sometimes from the camping field by the pub, invading the village for a few weeks. We heard about them, but it was too far along here for most of them to walk, they stayed far along, beyond the inlet, and went boating. My mother warned me, long ago, never to go near them and I never did.

She used to come with me when I was small, and show me how to do things. From her I learnt the secrets of the island, about the things to eat and the things that are bad to eat, making fire, how to take shelter, where to make a camp. She made me wash in the sea every day, wash me and my clothes, clean away mess, keep the beach tidy. Pumice, razor-shell, sponge, broke-toothed comb, washed-up toothbrush. She was bent over in a curve, like the pine trees which the wind has doubled up, and she leaned on me, more and more heavily. Now she is always inside, can't get out, stuck there inside like a lobster in its pot. I can't go in. I sit outside and sing to her, in my own way, not in talking, so perhaps she thinks it's the wind blowing her back again until she's upright and the long imprisonment is over.

Before, sometimes I could go indoors, into those closed spaces, and hold on for a while until I had to be out again. The panic feeling would be there within me, but I could tell it was far off, as far as the sea when it's out so far that the blue line looks like the bottom edge of the sky. Then it starts to roll in, closer, and gets faster as it gets nearer until it bursts over my head in a drowning chaos. Now I stay outside, so this can't happen unawares. I can make a roof, a shelter, anywhere, safe as a shell, but open.

When they came, my mother went in. Was it a spell, a curse, magic? Must have been, that's what I think. They used to say she was a witch, but she was just my mother. Hesketh put the eye on her, locked her up inside forever. Hesketh is so strong. Everyone is afraid of Her, the seals come when she calls, the fish shoal or flinch away, the birds hide. I hear that. I hear the vibration beneath Her feet wherever She walks, the thrumming of the things in the air which accompany Her. Kezia is Her daughter, but she is silent, she passes without disturbing the world. I am her slave.

Fitz

This place, Saltstreet, is unutterably desolate, makes me feel like an exile, castaway after the shipwreck of hopes. (Perhaps an exaggeration? We shall see.) On the journey I had to keep reminding myself that I'm not in such a bad state, compared with many others. At least I was in a uniform of sorts; I had all the passes, warrants, papers needed to prove me a traveller with a necessary journey, a citizen of this war-torn country with a right to move where I could in the dark world. I wasn't a displaced person, one of the stateless ones forbidden to cross borders, nor a bombed-out evacuee; this disaster was not of the same order. I'd escaped destruction, lost only possessions, my wounds will heal. But to be sent out of London to empty safety, away from my inheritance of leafy street and brick-bound park, is to be dispossessed of my birthright. (Everyone is the prince of their own place.) Since I've managed to remain based in the city throughout, it's a blow to my pride to desert it now.

As I sat on my suitcase in that lurching train corridor, shunted through the suburbs, I cursed Bradenham's over-scrupulous sense of honour. I curse it now. There's nothing *I* want less than a convalescent leave as the reward for being wounded on duty, if you can call it that. Old Brad will particularly dislike to be driven by anyone else; will miss my patient attendance outside the club long after midnight, my careful driving to spare her gout, my silent collusion in all her schemes, my resignation to the unofficial tasks of buying her cigarettes or posting her letters. No temporary replacement will be nearly so obliging, yet we are both condemned to suffer by her strong determination to treat her staff particularly well. This ridiculous trip into the unknown has only been authorised out of misplaced propriety.

I saw sooty bluebells on the embankment, lime trees budding in back gardens, women out in their yards in the evening sunshine, felt my eyes sting with tears. The only excuse is the length of that journey in foul air, my bad foot continually kicked or trodden on. There were unexpected pauses when the train stopped for so long that it seemed unlikely ever to move again, then it set off so abruptly that everyone fell over. The usual grumbling was interspersed with songs, flirtation, an occasional fight. Hardly any women were onboard, and very few civilians, as the atmosphere indicated. When daylight failed, with only glow-worm lamps to illuminate the compartments, the corridors dim too, solid masses of travellers in unlikely heaps slept as though comforted by gentle nursery nightlights.

The train ran on through the unknown darkness, stopping rarely now, rattling faster than it had seemed to by day, with an urgent force so that the sleepers were shaken or rolled about as they groaned and snored. Some time during the night I lost any sense of myself as I had been, abandoned myself to nothingness, perhaps slept. It was delayed shock of some sort, maybe, that bad moment on the train, one of those aftermaths which suddenly assail people who have been rescued; whatever it was, it shook me. Early on, when the war was just starting, when I was half-crazy with anxiety about other people, I never felt my own self in jeopardy. When the blitz was on, night after night, London in flames, no sleep for anyone, everyone on edge, I was solid. I drove through raids coolly, fast in the darkness, delivered my boss where she needed to be, carried messages back and forth through it all, saw bad sights, yet slept well. My appetite was not altered, nor my idea of myself.

11

Now, I suppose I'm 'rattled', as they call it, though why it should get me like that on the train, I've no idea. While I was doing that very ordinary job, nothing unusual about it, I suppose I kept myself going by various stratagems; I distracted myself by reading all the time, everything; I thought about the things I read, as though they were more real, mattered more than what was around me; I kept the boredom and fatigue at bay by living in my head. During my time off, of course, it was different; like anybody else I have my entertainments, my rewards. But the idea of such comforts seemed very remote during that long night journey. I suppose I'd made my walls which kept certain thoughts in and others out, and being hurt had shaken them down.

The numbness of my leg disturbed me; I struggled to stand up. Another passenger, an airman, head lavishly bandaged, amiably passed me my stick.

'I suppose we're lucky not to be taken round the schools and shown off like pet monkeys,' he remarked. 'One chap I knew had to lecture about his experiences to a lot of kids.'

'That would be even worse,' I admitted.

For these kind people, I could not then imagine them, have volunteered to take in a convalescent officer. (Instead, they've received me, a no-doubt-unpleasant surprise.) Or are we simply billeted without mercy on people unfortunate enough to live in the country? On the way, I kept wondering what the others would be like; I pictured our destination as a country-house hotel turned into a glorified nursing home for the duration.

A very drunk corporal squeezed his way along the corridor asking repeatedly, in a fruity music hall posh voice, 'Enjoying the war?' Nobody answered, except to bawl 'shut up' at him. I answered within myself that the war had stolen my youth. There are many things it's too late for me to do now, or not in the carefree way of the young. Surely it's part of the condition of youth to be unaware of it, not to worry about time? None of us can ever feel like that again. We can't wait, so this sudden posting away seems like the final blow to hopes I had – of the slow opening of the passion-flower as the sun warms it.

Without any warning the train stuttered to a halt, whistles blew, shouts on the platform told us sickies to disembark. There was no sign yet of dawn, but its welcome chill filled the damp air. The torches of the porters made a curious fan-vaulting pattern on the brick wall of the station, like some light-dance of local significance, impenetrable to outsiders. After long delay, with much resultant complaining, we were called out of the crowd by name, allotted seats in the usual huge military cars with covered lights. One of my companions was the head-injury airman, who kept apologising that his luggage had to rest on our laps. The car-smell of sweat-polished leather, old tobacco, brilliantine, seemed curiously homelike. From the station we were driven to our destinations in utter darkness. A passenger disappeared at each stop, taken one by one into barely glimpsed houses, until only I remained. It was very silent after the last whispered 'Cheerio', the heavy thud of the door. The car crawled along, shrouded lights showing nothing ahead but a dislocated sliver of ground, while the driver peered forward, the peak of her cap almost touching the windscreen.

'Lost?' I asked, after a while.

She didn't bother to answer, but said, 'What happened to you, then?'

I told her.

'In pain?'

'A bit of cramp, now.'

After stopping to consult the map again she drove on, saying lightly, 'They have sent you to the end of the world! It's out across the marsh – never been there before. Aren't you the lucky one, to get a place by the sea?'

'I don't much like the sea.'

I fell asleep. When she put me out in a sort of farmyard, she surprised me by saying, 'Good luck!' The house door opened into light; two women took me in. I thought in my state of glittering exhaustion that they were like a pair of tall herons ushering me through some door of perception.

One of the herons brought me tea on that first morning (day before yesterday? day before that?), staring at me with an open curiosity which made her seem closer to child than woman. It's still hard to tell her age; more than it seems, perhaps. I asked her name, which she told me with great seriousness: 'Kezia'. She says it oddly, like a foreign person, emphasising the I. After she'd gone I hopped over to the window (appropriately small and cottagey) to look out on my isolation. It took me a moment to believe. The rush-screened lane along which we'd driven in the darkness is a causeway, winding bridge rather than road, across half-flooded marshland where narrow water-courses make elaborate meanders between islets of mud-rooted reeds in a wild pewter sky-reflecting maze. Inland, at distance, low hills are grey-green, ochre-edged, with church tower among low houses as expected – all very English, no doubt very pretty.

The room itself is like the cottage bedroom in a fairytale, where the rescued boy wakes to survey the pale, tranquil room flooded with light in which the beautiful daughters of the house will heal him, until he is strong again. (This effect is slightly marred by the dustiness, which is the finishing touch to an air of general neglect, quite unlike the neat housewifely skills of the women in the stories.) *Full fathom five …* goes the song in my head. It's come back again, the refrain of loss which took so long to silence last time, but its music sounds different now. As before, I answer it with the vision of a hotel in a foreign city, with long shutters opening out of all the rooms onto elaborate wrought-iron balconies. At dusk people come out to admire the lights of the harbour below. By day, striped awnings are pulled low to keep the rooms cool. It is quiet, would be dull but for its beautiful setting. This is a place where lost souls might wait until they were allowed home. My talisman presently stills the old sad music.

I wondered what the hell I was doing here; I am none the wiser yet. By the end of the first day Hesketh, the one who is an artist, still had not appeared. Her daughter took lunch to her in the studio on a tray. By her manner I inferred the mother to be famous perhaps, difficult certainly. There was a wordless admonishment to be respectful when we should meet. Meanwhile, I was shown around the place, this world's end I have come to. It doesn't even have a name of its own: Saltstreet is miles away, a long circumnavigation, either inland across the marsh to the lane which eventually leads to the coast road, from which another lane turns off down to the quay with its few houses (not worth the effort, Kezia implies), or along the beach and up the waterway by boat. The inland church tower we can see is the second church in an old, landlocked Saltstreet, which has long lost its surrounding village – but Saltstreet is the closest named place, the only name.

This house was once a boatshed; that's why the road leads out to it across the marsh. It was bought, converted, used as a summer studio by one Giles, some well-off artist friend of Hesketh. (He lets them live in it because he never comes here himself, apparently.) It was rather smartly done up once, in about 1927 perhaps – there's a tidetable bearing this date stuck up on the mirror – but never again. By the time they arrived here a decade ago to borrow it as a temporary sanctuary, it must already have acquired the slightly shabby, apologetic air of a holiday cottage which is too cold in winter and really – from the owner's viewpoint – rather too far from London. There are enough books for years of rainy weekends.

In the single big downstairs room the paintwork was once cream, trimmed with pale grey, to match the thickly glazed striped chintz, square chrome clock, Rayburn like a shiny motor car. (This once-modish, obviously expensive renovation perhaps explains why the bedroom, though very small, is perfectly comfortable.) There's an indoor bathroom too, downstairs. It has a black bath, geometric patterns of tiles in black, white or looking-glass, curtains with square-headed people in Egyptian profile marching naked towards their ablutions. When I cleaned my teeth, I found the water was salt.

The daughter, Kezia, took me out into the so-called yard, a hard-trodden mud island where cars can turn round at the end of the causeway, surrounded by odd little outbuildings or windbreaks. We walked round the side of the house – not widdershins, I hoped – and there was the sea unexpectedly at my feet. The tide was very high, she told me. By evening the water would retreat, almost out of sight. It's impossible not to think of her in this setting as some sort of sea-creature: nothing as ethereal as a nymph, but perhaps a selkie, or half-marine sprite. She has those watchful yet fear-free eyes, wide with her constant gazing, which one imagines such creatures to possess; an innocent air of everyday strangeness, as though to disappear beneath the sea would be perfectly natural to her. There is also something so absolutely ordinary about her matter-of-fact conversation, entirely based on our immediate surroundings, that she seems quite commonplace – indoors, at least.

Hesketh, her mother, who I notice often glances at us out of her window, omnipresent in her distanced silence, could pass more convincingly as a sea-goddess, or the personification of a river. Nothing about her contradicts this impression; there is something opulent about her, yet the grandeur is eccentric, like a fallen genius perhaps. I recognise her power, unquestionably, but it is not consistent. Neither of them are comfortable neighbours.

Kezia

Our refugee – Fitz, she told me to call her, straight away – shocked me. I had expected a romantic figure – a Shakespearean character such as those I knew the world must be filled with – princely changelings, royal sheep-herders, heroic castaways – undefined by their apparent gender or occupation yet – beneath their workaday disguises – recognisable to the initiate. But the limp which had been mentioned was pronounced – not a rolling sea-gait or a Byronic sway – not a literary limp – only a pained stiff shuffle awkwardly favouring one leg. She appalled me that first morning, when she laboriously descended to the kitchen at nearly lunchtime – wearing a battered greatcoat as a dressing gown over red pyjamas – unhooked her bandaged hand from its paisley sling – groped in her pocket – triumphantly produced an old brass cigarette case. I mutely refused the offer of a strangely mangled cigarette.

'Does your ma smoke? No? I'd better go outside then.'

She picked out a cigarette with her lips – heaved herself up – snatched her stick just at the moment when her downfall seemed inevitable – swooped at the door with a piratical flourish.

Outside, the lighting of the cigarette with a battle-scarred lighter was another ceremony, which I watched with fascination. Fitz stared bleakly about her – short hair whipping into her eyes – as though she hoped a taxi might come along. I realised she was not so very much older than me – enough to be different – those crucial years. We walked round to the seaward side. When she saw the sea suddenly like that she gave the same cry of recognition with which I always greeted the returned ocean. Her eyes watered too, but she said it was the wind. I offered my arm for her to lean on as we went back in, but she said no. We talked very little to start with. I knew she was miserable – I wanted to show her the beauties of the place – but she couldn't walk far enough to see much. Even the food – which I thought must be an improvement on what she usually got – roused no enthusiasm, although she was polite. (As a treat I'd made fried eggs on truffle pâté with parsnip fritters – admittedly the pâté was excavated from an ancient tin – but still very rich.)

Haltingly, she asked all her questions – some of them I could not answer. Most of all, I wanted to interpret Hesketh to her, to be sure she understood Hesketh as a different kind of being. I explained that Hesketh hadn't intended to keep us as hermits enclosed from the world – I am almost sure – only to come to a place of safety temporarily – shelter there from threatening disaster. But the days passed – the years passed – the war came and stranded us. We had nowhere else to go – they expected an invasion right here in Saltstreet and for a while we were forbidden to leave – yet threatened with having the house requisitioned. Next the area was suddenly declared open again – suitable to receive the bombed-out and frightened-off from elsewhere. It would have been madness to move then – we were used to it now – it was home. Fitz agreed – most politely – with everything I said.

I am an elemental being. My emotions are simple, with the strength of their purity. If I love – or hate – I do not try to conceal it – nor is there any need to voice it. My states of heart exist, undeniably – I accept them like weather. I played chess with Fitz – showed her things about the place – watched her as she read for hours hunched in the breezy window seat – never questioned beyond my own sympathy. For me, there had always been this centre – deftly conjured by my left-handed mother – a certainty which nothing would gainsay. But for our visitor – I kept reflecting – there was no one to make any security – no such comfort. I still knew this rawly enough to feel sorry – so sorry – that night she arrived, reeling in from the darkness as though the sea had just cast her up. (Hesketh drily reminded me that our guest had only come from blacked-out London, rather than a Greek island – a contrast not quite so striking.)

That first evening when Hesketh came down to supper she stared at Fitz – who was wearing her corduroy trousers and navy-surplus roll-neck – almost rudely. I thought it was as though she recognised her – or something about her – which was a surprise – though not an unpleasant one. There were questions – naturally – to which I listened with anxiety in case Fitz could not remember the answers. (She had told me – quite matter of factly – that the injury had given her amnesia – not completely – she added before I could make up her story for her – only about what had happened to her then.) But Fitz knew the name of her company – she was certainly an officer – she knew what had happened to her and her car – though not as an eye-witness.

'Did you get a knock on the head?' Hesketh asked, with interest.

'Don't know, can't remember,' Fitz said – they both roared with laughter. 'Sorry, I've caught hospital humour. No, no head injury. Just shock.'

'It will pass.'

'I certainly hope so; it's most disconcerting.'

Hesketh said that same spell to Fitz, the first night she was with us – *be not afraid*. We were eating at the kitchen table – close to the Rayburn – drinking wine. There was a sudden thump of wind against the house, and Fitz jumped up in alarm – spilling – forgetting her injuries in her fright. Hesketh put out a hand – took Fitz's arm commandingly – spoke her soothing words about the island's noises. Fitz muttered an apology for her 'nerves' – awkwardly settled herself again – Hesketh patted her shoulder. I remembered that first night we were here – I still felt Hesketh's power – believed in her – just as I had when I was a child.

Fitz

I have learnt many things very quickly at Saltstreet, especially not to say 'Mrs' Hesketh. This was the mistake I made when I first addressed her, which caused her to raise one red circumflex eyebrow sardonically. My elaborate apologies were accepted graciously, as though the mistake had been merely gauche. Then, when I pointed out that I couldn't have known in advance unless someone had told me, she laughed, clapped me on the shoulder, agreed. Since then, I am in favour (which is a relief); I gained some kind of promotion by that boldness. But this odd household is far more tolerant than a conventional one, where any attempts to conform would be doomed by my differentness – which is barely noticed here.

In the first few days I found out that drinking water for boiling comes out of the rainwater butt, or else has to be carried from the spring head across the marsh, although there are sometimes bottles of Malvern water on the table. I mastered the routine of leaving my requests for cigarettes or stamps in an envelope, with the appropriate money or coupons, for a woman called Mrs Dews to collect when she makes the deliveries – but so far I have never seen her. No one comes out along the causeway; the post and carrier's deliveries are left on a wooden milk-platform by an old stile on the inland side of the marsh, as though we have the plague. I discovered that Kezia's long plait is called Rapunzel, so that when she shouts 'Wait! I'm just finishing Rapunzel' she's doing her hair. I understand that the tall knickerbocker-glory glass, with its accompanying card of St Francis preaching to the birds, is kept for catching the enormous spiders which lurk under the bath, to escort them from the house, and that *no other card or glass will do*.

I realise Kezia wants to be kind. She demonstrates this by taking me to see interesting insects, or letting me look through Benbow, her old telescope, at passing boats (of which there are few). I feel flattered by her confidences, as one is by those of unknown children, but in the same way, slightly nonplussed. She showed me the logbook which she has kept ever since they arrived here when she was eleven, recording the weather, the tide, the moon's phases. It is not scientific, but descriptive, with measurements she understood, such as: *waves – not high but definite; a dog would not want to swim through them*. From the sheds she produces, for my amusement, unrecognisable games in wooden boxes, rotten deckchairs, rubber boots, exhibits to me a possibly salvageable bicycle, an impossibly theatrical canoe, all kinds of beach paraphernalia, all very rusty and damp-smelling. My only escape from her solicitude is reading, she understands that; I call it work. But in truth, reading is my medicine, the only healing art which is good for me here.

In this briny temporary shelter I miss solid ground beneath my feet; we all walk on water. I'm more comfortable when I can imagine that the land beneath is imprinted by many feet, on quarry tiles over monastery floor above Roman pavement across older stones, which in turn stood on once-ploughed land made sacred by the patina of long usage. Above the mosaic floor, line upon line, stacks the narrative debris of people's lives, treasures and rubbish casually intermingled, up to the level where I now stand making my footprint forever. London carries all that in its ground, inevitably, impossible not to feel it; there are still the old orchard trees in the gardens, the hedgerow boundaries, the good rich soil speckled with human relics beneath the paving stones. Here, we seem to hover in a wilderness, entirely alone in no-time, unsupported

23

by the past, invisible to the future. Even the cobbles on the beach make me homesick for streets.

As I observe the way of life here, I realise that this week has been exactly like last and there is no reason why next should be any different. My hosts, the herons, know nobody, have no wireless, hear no news; like enclosed nuns or desert-island dwellers they remain untouched by outward things, do not miss them. Kezia, I discover, never went to school, nor does she have any work other than looking after her mother. She is extremely well-educated, but without any experience. I feel like a conquistador lurching onto the virgin sands, cutlass in teeth, bible in hand, infections on my boots – though I'm a most unwilling colonist. While I wish the islanders nothing but good, all I desire is to return to my own civilisation.

My memory doesn't seem to be patchy, except that I have no recollection of my injury, which the doctors told me was quite common, nothing to worry about. (If they had a place in the mind which was blank, remained blank however often it was revisited, would they 'not worry'? Perhaps not.) I lie awake testing my memory, walking across the familiar landscape, mapping it, beating the bounds, making sure no spinney or tree-stump has escaped from the boundaries into nothingness. It has occurred to me that if there were odd gaps, bomb-holes, mine-craters, I might not know; those sudden lurches into the void might perhaps only be noticeable if one could recall everything exactly as it was before. So I set off again, testing, exploring, revisiting, yet feeling I prove nothing.

Nobody is near who can corroborate my story. So I wonder, was Granfa wounded at Guadalajara? (*Full fathom five...*) Or was it in Granada? These minor confusions are not even lapses of memory I would normally notice, but any

24

forgetfulness has acquired a disproportionate significance. To return to the same point repeatedly is obviously not helping my wits, concentration, or temper. It's the stranger's place to accept hospitality civilly, with grace; I remind myself of this. I am learning how to play chess with Kezia, who is evidently very good at it. My favourite is the knight's move.

Crambo

I saw Kezia first. She was smaller then, almost still a child. It was the only time I met someone on the beach accidentally, I almost ran into her. She was waving at me, as though my arm-flailing as I scurried along was meant as a greeting to her. I tacked on past and away, taken aback that my look-out had failed, so that she'd seen me all unwary beetling up and down the dunes. When the animals lose their caution, they die. I had seen her too though, and she was like nothing, no one, I'd ever glimpsed before. And behind her, the boatshed was open, there were people there, the shutters taken down and window glass showing, furniture inside, things I did not recognise or understand were in there.

I watched them, for many days I hid and watched them. She was the child, daughter, of the other one, Hesketh, who was a powerful being. They lived there. I brought them tributes, flowers, firewood, fish, in secret, left on the steps down to the beach. This was propitiation, not welcome. I thought of trying to drive them away. How long would they stay? Why were they there? What could they want in my place?

One day, when I went to the steps with a handful of oysters, there was an old wooden crate, a driftwood box, already sitting there, with a square tin bedded in it, a blue and silver thing of incredible intricate beauty, new and shiny. I smelt food inside, and could see no trap, so I snatched it and took it back to my camp. Inside, there was silver paper, inside that, dark brown blocks like the hardest smooth wood, too strong to bite but sweet, sweet. I lay there all day, licking. Taste. There had been such sweet before, but long long ago. Now it was all salt, or the sharp fruit-sweet of blackberries.

That night it was full moon, and I danced on the beach and sang to her in the sky, and felt the sweetness surging in my body like a current speeding along old deep channels. My hymn flew along the light-path on the water and blew the crazed clouds about the sky. It was intensely cold, but I danced naked as the moon prefers, and felt no chill, only ecstasy. I was ill after, but it was with yearning, not cold. I went to sleep at nights snuffing the tin, clutched it for comfort as I lay and shivered all day. As soon as I could drag myself out I crawled along the beach, to the boathouse, to beg for more.

They gave me so much, both what I needed and what was too rich for me. They even gave me my name. I was just called Dumby before. Except my mother used to call me something else when I was little, but I can't remember it now. 'Dumb Crambo' means making you understand without talking, which was what I used to do before they taught me. So now it's just Crambo. It was seeing the two of them talking to each other *about me* which first made me understand properly about speech. As I sat on the steps, sucking on a little black and white stone, all sweet, until the drool ran down my chin, I realised that they were singing to each other as I sang to the moon, and making a reply, an answering. I thought only my mother could do that with me, but they expected to as well. It was this, not the sweets, not Kezia, which made me able to learn their language. I think I only learnt it after a fashion, in a Crambo-version.

In return, I showed her everything, where the seals are, where to gather the best shellfish, harvest the seaweed, find birds' nests, where the sun strikes first and lingers last all year, how to be cool or warm, which stars show at the different seasons, where it's safe to swim, where we mustn't go, everything. All my silence she was welcome to, since I could speak to her now. I let her see my things, the patterns, the boats in the ground. Sometimes she helped me to make pebble spirals, stone cairns, things the sea likes. She understood about finding all white stones, or all black ones, or the purple-lined shells, red mottled blue cockles, for making the patterns just as the sea does, writing the sea on the sand.

I kept no secrets for myself, held nothing back. The whole of my island, its essence and heartwood, seemed a small enough gift to make her. My reward was that she was pleased. What they took from me, my kingship, my place, they did not even want. They hardly knew they had taken it, since I gave everything freely. But I felt the loss. There seemed to be less of me left, some diminishment of Crambo, and I did not know how to get it back.

Kezia

Perhaps when Hesketh decided to bring us here – to the place friends could offer as a solution – perhaps she had no idea how remote it was – how extreme. A lighthouse could hardly have been more removed from the hub of the world. For those unknown people it had represented a contrast as marked as possible – the game of a different life – perhaps a decadent choice – but they soon gave it up. Yet it suited some instinct in her to withdraw – seek a sanctuary far away – be hidden. I suppose she knew that in wilderness places – strangely beautiful – not everything can tolerate living – but those things that can adapt thrive there as nowhere else.

Nothing grows beyond the marsh at the sea margin – no garden flowers. There are plants – salt-resistant sand-dwellers – juicy-leaved succulents which inch across the beach bearing their own water – strange yellow waxy poppies – teazel-like thistles blue all over – marram grass on the dunes parted like hair by the wind over this way then that – sea lavender covering the marsh in a dense forest of rattling dried immortelles. Only on the earth bank of the sea wall – running inland to contain the marsh waters – does something like ordinary grass grow – but it is still different – oddly textured. In summer sometimes a small convolvulus – white or faintly pink-striped – wriggles tenuously out across the sandy paths, but it soon fades. There's a compact pincushion plant with little white flowers – sometimes – unexpectedly prickly to touch. I used to know the names of all of these – I knew everything like that – learnt out of books.

Inland – even just across the marsh – most things will grow – with persuasion. On that side there are even fruit trees – beans in gardens – herb bushes and flowering climbers.

Perhaps a little wind-beaten – a little salt-singed. The further you go inland the more fertile the ground becomes – green saturates the view – seeps up from the horizon. It's not bleak country – once the sea's influence fades – but to me it hasn't the power – the physical pull of the edge.

I remember the years before the war – before Fitz came – as happy, in a cool ethereal way. It was not a solid happiness which a child could cling to – but as light and incorporeal as a draught – a chill air blowing delicately through some unstopped gap. It seems a melancholy sort of happiness – now – but I breathed it eagerly then. Hesketh made everything into an adventure. To her, Saltstreet was just an interlude – stopgap temporary lodgings – but she noticed that it coincided with my most significant childhood years – which were not going to be ordinary. After the shock of arrival – before the war and the whisky sent her a little mad – it was a charmed life. I was educated with anecdotes and charades – word games and reference books – by playing records and reading plays. Hesketh could transform any occasion into an event – lunch on the beach became not only a picnic – a treat – but a celebration of summer – a seasonal ritual – a pleasant sacrifice to beneficent gods. Indeed, Hesketh could make anything – draw anything – invent anything – when I had her attention.

There were times when she vanished – either working too hard to notice me, or otherwise remote. I was never lonely – certainly not bored. I had my log – my observations to make and record – my collections to catalogue and augment – my rounds of the beach and marsh to take. Every day there was something new brought to our door by the sea. At night, I studied the stars through brass Benbow's lens – imagined finding a new comet. Soon after we arrived, I understood the tides – not only as my books explained them – with tide

30

tables and diagrams – but in my body. The people born on the coast arrive with the incoming tide – only die when it turns to the ebb – that's their way. It's the same for me too – a rhythm of living or dying – a surge in the blood which tells the time. The moon is my sun – the measurer – the heavenly dial. I know why people anciently threw their sacrifices into the water – sea, lake or river – not to placate but to worship. Crambo does this for us. He makes things for the sea – his sand-patterns, his stone-piles – because he thinks the sea likes it – to give pleasure. Yet when the tide comes high and throws his efforts about – engulfs his offering – he seems perversely delighted.

I could understand when Hesketh withdrew into her work – preoccupied – sometimes silent – for days at a time – though with an effort she could rouse herself from her trance if I needed anything, and ask how I was. It was not that Hesketh was dreamy – not vaguely contemplating some inner vision from which she could be recalled, apologising, to the 'real' world – an absent-minded artist. No, her absorption was fierce – absolute – interruptions were fought against with intense seriousness – any infraction deeply resented. I respected this, and it did not concern me. When the lighthouse beam of her attention turned on me, for as long as it lasted the illumination could seem almost too bright.

The other times were darker. When she could not work – and could not emerge from it either – I felt she was not herself. Sometimes she wailed like an old sailor at a wake, rocking herself back and forth until her teeth chattered. Sometimes she drank herself insensible – I would find her passed out on the sofa – impossible to rouse. Sometimes when she was drunk she would make terrible scenes with me – or rather, at me, since I did not participate. Then would come the litany of how

I looked like my father – might well *be* like him – so cold and silent sitting there guarding my emotions while she – look at her now – gave and gave getting nothing back. Afterwards she said she remembered nothing about it, and of course I said the same. It made no difference to my admiration – if anything it increased my opinion of her, rather as a really violent storm reminds one to respect the sea – which is capable of that extremity. For I was – in the same way – slightly afraid of her.

I knew Hesketh was powerful – unpredictable – damaged in some essential mechanism, yet still intensely gifted. As a child I was awed by her – as I grew up nothing happened to adjust my way of seeing to a more workaday view. I had no illusions to lose – the worst was inextricable from the best. Once – one summer when I was a child – I sat in the studio on a little chair, drawing one of my charts. The sun was slanting in through the windows in great triangular blocks of solid light – wedges of brightness delineating the dusty element of air. Hesketh slowly walked along the room – ceremonially – her linen overall draped like a processional robe. Where she walked blue petals wafted about her head and fluttered down to mark her path. She moved through the flowery golden air unaware of her beauty. I realised after a moment that she was carefully carrying a vase of delphiniums – scabious – cornflowers – monkshood – which she had been painting – the blown flowers were dropping their petals in drifts around her. This glimpse of her glory was not diminished when she saw the blue confetti-trail on the floorboards behind her and exclaimed 'Blast!'

I wanted so much to show this – for Fitz to know her like this – when I heard them getting drunk together downstairs – still sitting at the kitchen table at midnight roaring with laughter. I knew how she would be later. Fitz – younger, no make-up to smudge, no tall hair-arrangement to descend – would just go red, get very gruff. Hesketh might not remain transcendent. I went down there in my dressing gown, still holding my book. They were planted there with their elbows among the plates – smoking indoors – drinking up a long-opened bottle of madeira. Hesketh's hair was not falling down – she had shaken it loose and it was spread magnificently across her shoulders in a dense copper-beech-leaf shawl. After they had asked kindly what I wanted – if they were being too noisy – if I wanted a hot drink – Hesketh said, 'Go back up to bed, darling, we'll try not to disturb you.' And I did.

One thing I couldn't understand was what Hesketh found funny about Fitz – at her own expense, not Fitz's, something amused her. Long before Fitz came we'd discussed the ghastly possibility of having an evacuee billeted on us – although we were so isolated, ill-equipped and eccentric that we were never included in such a scheme. Hesketh told me later that she'd written to someone she knew – in some organising organisation – offering a place for a wounded officer to convalesce by the sea. Perhaps it was to ensure we didn't get anything worse – in terms of numbers or variety – perhaps it was even more calculating. The unintentional sabotage of her schemes was the kind of thing which amused Hesketh – sometimes – especially if she'd tried to make some conventional gesture without success.

So Hesketh expected a hero – as sent for – and got Fitz instead. Hesketh had heard – where? how? – dreadful stories about evacuees sending their unwilling hosts mad with their feckless filthy ways – their idle freeloading. Compared with these characters Fitz's unfailing courtesy – her attempts to help when she could – her frequent thanks – made her a welcome stranger indeed. But there were also tales of ideal son-in-laws arriving ready-parcelled – to order – handsome, decorated, malleable – most unlike Fitz with her burly bohemian look – her louche theatrical air. (And she seemed so sad, so lost without her usual props.) The joke was on us – but (I think) Hesketh was also secretly relieved. When I saw her with Fitz there was something – an equality between them – a respectful comradeliness – which made me realise that they had more in common with each other than with me – some parity of vision I didn't share.

Crambo

The incomer, the other one, had no business here, it's not his place. He came to take her away, that's clear enough, but a poor limping thing like that, a runt, was hardly going to be good enough for a pearl like her. Never! I watched him, whenever he went out. I watched him going so slowly along with his big overcoat flapping like a scarecrow, always stopping to look at the sky, empty-headed idiot. If I had great leather boots like that I could walk better than that. He had a lighter, flame-at-will, like soldiers have, and I thought he probably had a pocket-knife, field-glasses, all the things those kinds of people have. Maybe a torch, maybe a gun, maybe a sword inside his stick. He tried to talk to me a few times, but I wasn't having any of that, why should I?

Sometimes Kezia went with him, held his arm like she sometimes held mine in the gale. I could see them talking. Hesketh sent for him, why else would he be here, so She wasn't going to set the dog after him. I had to be the dog myself this time. I watched them carefully as they sat down on the stile, and I thought that he didn't love her at all, not like me. He looked at her kindly enough, but with no storm in the eyes, as though she was just a clever child, no more. I didn't know how she felt about him, I couldn't see.

One time, one time it snowed in the night, it was a long time ago when I used to sleep under the log-shelter by the cottage sometimes, so I woke up dry. I saw the different light and I ran out onto the green to taste the flakes on my tongue. It was slow, floating snow, the sort that entangles in your eyelashes and makes crusts on your shoulders and across your neck, it tasted of nothingness. On the ground, footprints went as deep as into the softest sand, but stayed better, more clearly, so you could see where the birds had been, exactly which ones, and all the other animals' tracks. The lizards are my favourite, footprints with tail-trails, but they don't come out in the snow. I capered about, I disported myself with the snow, rolled in it, munched it, made my own marks in it.

When I came to the sea the beach wasn't different, it was the same, only snowed on. The sea was like me, it ate the snow, nibbling all along its edges where it turned into snow and sea both at once, taking some chunks of ice out to float in it, chinking in the waves. I sang to it. Kezia came out, dressed in all her clothes at once, she called to me, 'Crambo, aren't you cold?' and I yodelled and laughed. She ran down and took hold of my hand, she had gloves on, and we ran along the beach together so our footmarks showed it had been us, like prints in the sand but more so. After we'd gone nearly to the wishbone her breath ran out and she had to stop and bend over, she was laughing so much because of the snow, and I was laughing too.

If ever I felt sad about Kezia, I thought about that time, the pulling in different directions when we were running, the snow on her hair. There's a special name for a thing you keep in your head for ever like that, to take out and look at sometimes, and it's always there for you whenever you like, although you don't do it too often in case of wearing it away, a special word Kezia told me once, but I don't know what it is now.

When I see the wind moving across the marsh and the reeds shuffle together and shiver, sometimes there is almost no noise. But I hear, when I listen, voices blowing in my head, wailing and droning. I do not wish to hear anything, I prefer silence. The voices are not welcome, they torment me. I am afraid of them, afraid of Hesketh's black dog Ara, which looks at me.

I never told about the voices, not to Kezia, I only told her about the men in fort field by accident, I thought she knew already. I saw one of them on the beach the other day, you can always recognise them because they don't wear any trousers, their faces are like mine, all brown and polished flinty smooth, and sometimes they wear shining masks with crests, like plovers. He was sitting on his own on a rock doing up his shoe, his lace had broken and he was trying to knot it, they have a lot of laces all round their legs. I watched him fiddling with it in the still sunshine, bent over to reach, I didn't think he would see me but suddenly he twitched round and jumped up quickly, and went loping off, hurrying but staring behind him. I don't know why, I wouldn't have hurt him.

I didn't tell anyone about that, nor the urn burials, I do have some secrets but they're not my own to tell or keep. There's a field up behind the village called the gold field and once a long time ago they came and dug all it up to look for things, to take them away, but they didn't find much. I know where all the big pots are, all full of ashes and gold, but I'm not saying, they're not for digging up, they were buried same as in the churchyard. I find other things, things that were left behind but no one will come back for them now. That's different. Once I put my hand down a rabbit hole and pulled out a pot like the ginger beer jar my ma kept on the windowsill, except it was dirty and all burnished in one place from the rabbits squeezing past. Inside were black discs squashed together like a lump of sea-coal, coins, old coins, Kezia told me, I gave them to her.

And I gave her the little glass bottle I found, whole, under a horned poppy bush in the sand, all blue and white swirls like the inside of a special stone, but with a bloom on it, a rainbow lustre like the sea has when petrol cans float in. It had a tall neck, with lugs and a curly loop of glass like a lizard's tail round its middle. It was pretty, but I didn't want to keep it. I prefer the other kind of things which the sea brings, sometimes the sea makes them or sometimes after they've gone in the sea it changes them. In the sea there's everything.

I try not to listen to the words, the voices inside, but other times there are different sounds from within, whistles, loud clicks, thick boiling noises, bubbling as I chew. The sea has got inside my head, come down my ears and filled up the tubes, surges about in the hollows, that's what I think. If I shake my head I hear it sloshing about inside, so it's as though my ears are under the water, all the time, and what's above doesn't sound right down here. Other times my head pokes out for a bit, outside noises come clear over the water, and I can hear them for a while. Seals can close their ears when they dive, and their nostrils. I wish I was a seal.

At night sometimes I think of them out there on their sandbank, all warm in a heap, tails overlapping heads, chin on flank, flippers spread, the whole crew of them safe asleep. What if there were other Crambos, and we all lay down to rest together at darkness? There couldn't be, though, there's only Crambo.

Fitz

Hesketh asked me one morning what I wanted. It was about a week ago. We were lounging outside on the bench that faced seaward, in some rare thin sunshine. I don't know why she had emerged from the studio but she was there, smoking one of my cigarettes with the charming air of an inexpert connoisseur.

'I want to be well enough to go back to London,' I said. I heard my voice thicken with urgency, my desire wreathed about me like pungent smoke.

'Oh, you will soon,' said Hesketh lightly. 'I expect you've got someone waiting for you there,' she added, as though it was a matter of course.

'Yes. Not really,' I said, indistinctly. 'I mean, I hope so.'

'So of course you need to get home. What else?'

But I couldn't tell her, although she might have understood. Instead, I admitted that I was worried I might not walk well again. For some reason her off-hand avowal that I'd be running by midsummer cheered me more than any medic's bracing reassurance. She added that swimming, when the weather was warm enough, would help. Swimming worked like magic, she said, but added, 'You'll always be able to tell when it's going to rain. Most useful.'

After this, Hesketh has made strange potions, like intense cold tea, out of various poisonous-looking weeds which I think – with grass-grit in my teeth – taste of a green grave. She calls them encouraging names such as heal-all, bone-mend, swift-foot. Also, she produced The Embrocation (as it is reverently known), some sort of fisherman's lineament or balm which smells eye-wateringly of peppermint and the North Sea. Since it comes in a large tin like saddle-soap or turpentine, I was suspicious enough to resist at first, suggesting they should recaulk their sou'westers with it instead. But I have to admit that the burn as I rub it in is amply worth it for the unknitting of my creaking muscles, which have troubled me with twitches in the night. Every day I go for a walk, not for pleasure, but persevering. Kezia tells me there is improvement.

Most things are in the present tense now, a curiously empty feeling. There are no obviously differing days of the week, no dates to be noticed except after calendar computation, no focus on the hours' unclocked passing. The past seems strangely distanced, on the other side of the blank space of non-memory, yet the future is also separated off by a similar, though more nebulous, impassable emptiness. In this timeless state Hesketh seems oddly reassuring; despite her unpredictability, she is always the same. When I spoke to her of the timelessness of the place she turned to geology, of which she knows nothing.

This coast is crumbling, she told me with satisfaction, though not as badly as 'round the corner', where the current takes a sharp turn round some gravelly shoulder of land. Round there, houses fall into the sea like teeth tipping unexpectedly over the lip, leaving a startling gap. Round there (warming to her theme) the cliff itself has fissures which you can step across to stand on a grassy island, separated from the mainland by a crack which will imperceptibly open until the unsupported pillar crashes down, a tall white-uniformed guardsman fainting at attention, with the grass-green busby still on. A deliciously risky fairground ride sensation, to leap across the dark crack in the turf, balance for a moment on the solid-seeming peninsula which is so imperceptibly a drifting island, dodge back just in time.

Unthinking picnickers near the cliff-edge...

Here it's flat, below sea-level even, behind the dunes where the marsh makes a water meadow to hold the tidal overflow. Inundation is commonplace. But the sea creeps ever further in. Hesketh told me that the boathouse once stood on a creek, half a mile back from the highest tides, behind a whole Sahara of dunes and sand-plains. There was a bridge to seawards; in a time before anyone remembers sheep grazed out where the seals now swim.

'Do the churchbells ring underwater?' I asked.

'Oh, yes. And Lyonesse rises up on misty nights, with lights to be glimpsed from the shore.'

'Like the seagulls "who still, it's said, hover over the lost island of Atlantis".' (I suppose I was rather drunk, misquoting poetry to relative strangers.)

'Those stories are all *true*,' Kezia said, with passion.

'Of course they are,' we both answered instantly. 'But old,' Hesketh added, 'old stories...'

Hesketh either paints like a woman in a trance, keeping vigil in her studio, hardly emerging, or behaves like a townswoman on a bucolic holiday, making the most of wild flowers, log fires, sunsets, local cooking ingredients. The rest of the country may be enveloped in war anxieties, but she inhabits a different place. I gather that it was like this throughout Kezia's childhood, when Hesketh was either the best of companions, or absent. I feel that Kezia and I both are always hoping she will come down, waiting like courtiers for her pleasure, for her to dispose of as she thinks best. I like her, even though she seems mildly amused by me; her worldly, comradely air is easier than Kezia's breathless expectancy.

Kezia often tells me about the things I will be able to do when I can walk further. (I don't say that I will then be back in

London.) Over the marsh, beside the great wool church of old Saltstreet with its high tower that was once a beacon to bring the ships in, she informs me there is a green with a few houses still surrounding it. One is the old vicarage, long closed up; one is the row of semi-derelict cottages where Crambo's mother lives, sometimes with her crazy sister who comes over from the village proper to visit. The last dilapidated house, which stands a little separate from the others, has been for rent since before the war; Kezia thinks the weather must have penetrated it by now. This deserted hamlet seems to Kezia an encouraging goal to reach. As I gain my bearings, at least by hearsay, the mysteries of the place swirl nearer; I grasp our absolute isolation, Kezia's separateness from the commonplace. I begin to well understand how these things have come about.

It's not that I can't see the beauty of it – it is terribly beautiful. But the isolation is so complete that she clings to the living things she sees here; the seals seem friendly companions, the birds' good augury is that we are not alone in the world. I start to perceive our fellow travellers in the same way, as prisoners name the beetles on their cell floor. Yesterday as I was resting, propped on the steep bank of the seawall like a chorister in a pew, an owl flew slowly past me just at shoulder-height. In the violet half-light of dusk its colour glowed brightly orange, unavoidably reminiscent of marmalade – indeed, of a winged marmalade cat. As it passed it turned its clock-faced head to meet my eyes with a stare of unblinking outrage. I loved that owl. I watched it while the light lasted, as it methodically criss-crossed the marsh, hunting, with a silent rolling glide. Its existence gives me a sort of illogical hope.

When I met a heron a few days before, standing on the bank of one of the rivulets, not fishing but apparently contemplating the sky, I bowed to it. I think of it as almost my height, which can't be so, but it was tall, hauntingly coloured, dignified. It looked at me with an expression I couldn't help reading as mild reproof, opened its drooping wings like a magician's cape, rose up into the sky with slow, flopping wingbeats of great power. I watched it fly off, quite low, its neck crooked into that stylised Japanese curve, to land in a less invaded spot. The presence of wild things provides sudden delights, but they make strange elusive companions for Kezia. I think that she accepted me into the household immediately, as though I was a badger which had been hurt in a trap, in front of whom no constraint was necessary. But perhaps I am also – who? All of her other friends are people from books.

Apart from these fictional comrades, Kezia has other strange company, too. A field abutting the marsh inland which always lies fallow, too bumpy to be any use, was evidently the site of a Roman fort. (This makes us all feel less alone, perhaps.) Kezia showed me the plan of it in one of her books, the outline of the turf-covered walls still discernible if one knows where to look. Nobody ever goes there. It was excavated in the last century by the local vicar, yielded a few coins, a legionary's sandal, some pot-sherds. I sometimes stand in the searing wind, staring at the rough field, trying to visualise the garrison about their chilly duties. Or as I lie in the bath, now I can lever myself in and out, while condensation drips cold rain on the angular profiles marching past, I think of the Commander's bath-house warmed under the mosaic floor to almost foreign heat.

'Was there a Roman road?' I asked Kezia.

'Oh, yes, a famous one. Something Street, that's why Saltstreet. At night you can hear them marching along it.'

I listened, I listen for the crash of hobnail on paviour, inviting the company of ghosts, but it never comes. Crambo, they tell me, meets them all the time, but he doesn't notice the difference. Until now, I realise, he has been Kezia's only other neighbour.

One day last week on one of my painful walks, the geese came over, approaching with their strange sound like an army clapping its gloved hands in muffled time. They streamed over; the leader of the V-formation dropped back while another moved smoothly forward to take its place at the apex of their flowing triangle, in perfect symmetry. No bomber squadron could equal that unforced manoeuvre. The old gold reflection of the low sun on the rivulets of the marsh made it almost too bright to look across, a garden inlaid with gilded paths. Inland, the hills were already dusky, as though the dark emanated from them. Little lights were starting to show from far-off cottages like a scene on a card from the days before blacking out, depicting the lamp in the window to signify homecoming, safe harbour, warm hearth. Out there on the rickety causeway, far outside, condemned to look in from the storm-threatened sea, I have never felt such a sense of exclusion, seen such chill beauty.

I returned, walking carefully, concentrating on setting my foot straight. The idea of my London stood before me like a glittering mirage. I thought for some reason of getting off the bus in Russell Square, walking through to the British Museum, the charcoal braziers outside with their winter scent of roast chestnuts, the tea shops where people (even now) would be sitting, deciding to go to a show or a concert or maybe the cinema ... I imagined the warm sensation of belonging which would envelop me as I thawed my hands in my pockets on the little paper bag of blackened chestnuts, considered my many choices. I thought of the times when I had seen or done something which seemed to remain with me yet: a concert at the National Gallery whose music still sounded unfading; a play at the Old Vic which echoed on. The vast illusion glimmered there in my mind, distant as the stars which were just beginning to make themselves visible. Homesick, cherishing my sickness, I plodded on.

In the dark yard I paused to have a last cigarette before I went in. As I was lighting it, I heard a noise which made my hair stir on my head, a *howl*. I was inside the house very fast, with the door shut behind me. Kezia looked up, gave me her slow solemn smile, laughed.

'Not wolves,' she said. 'It's Crambo. He's serenading me, listen.'

The cries continued, encircling the house; I realised he was calling 'Kesh-ar!' in a rising wail.

'Is it full moon or something?' I asked rudely.

'Maybe. I used to go and walk with him on bright nights, but now Hesketh won't let me. He's got rather difficult.'

Rather difficult. The unearthly sound was her name; he was summoning her out into that darkness in which light was still forbidden to be shown, to walk on the black beach with him, and she would have gone?

Crambo is my most obvious failure in learning the ways of Saltstreet. When I first saw him out of the window in his rusty trousers, dandy's white shirt billowing underneath his antique swallowtails, he struck me as a clown, a tragi-comic mountebank, juggler, tumbler. Up close, his wildness is more disturbing. He will not speak to me – I mean, he will not be spoken with; as soon as he sees me, he runs away. Yet as I walk along the marsh road I can see him, a black speck floating in the corners of my eyes, ducking, dodging among clumps of reeds, following me. On the beach too, if I go along a little way in either direction, I'm aware of him up in the dunes. His tall shell-encrusted hat emerges from the marram grass tufts like a submarine's periscope, or an hourglass-trickle of sand reveals his snaking passage down a sand-slide. This exasperates me, but there is something ludicrous about it too. *Outcast*, *edge-dweller*, *other*, I think; *it takes one to know one.*

The other thing which lowers my spirits is the incessant cold. Kezia told me about the summer, the marsh purple with sea-lavender flowers, the sand hot on the feet, the insistent sun. God knows, in London I've looked forward to spring, been glad to notice early daffodils, magnolias opening in proud front gardens, blossom in the squares. But here, scoured by the salt-bearing wind, people yearn for bud-break, hallucinate green shoots where none yet are, search the sky for signs of spring. (I remember even the railway embankments in bloom on my journey, calculate how much later it might reach here. It must be May, well into May now; surely time for some semblance of summer to begin?) I long for more than the chilly greening of distant trees; I want heat to dry out my damp bones. To be warm, to drive out the cold embedded in my veins, has become my other obsession. At night, after cooking, the kitchen end of the main room becomes less chilly, not impossible to sit in uncoated; also there is a ritual hotwater-bottle filling which generates some steamy warmth before the icy ascent to bed. That is all.

Hesketh seems immune to the cold. She stalks about, sometimes impatiently warming her hands with the air of being forced to gratify a purely human necessity. There are certain immutable rules for her comfort, though: hot water ready for her evening bath, the lunch trays, a very effective paraffin stove in the studio. She observed that I was willing the summer to start; that was how I first saw inside her studio. The view made me realise that I had been here for several weeks without understanding the place's position, sea-centred, set on the extreme margin of the land, aligned with nothing man-made. The complete lack of humanity outside contrasts strangely with the interior of the room, which is no salt-scarred beach hut but a workshop dedicated to an individual imagination, a glimpse into one mind.

Everything in it has at some long-ago time been painted white; all the different woods of floor, window-frame, door, beam, have made their various whites. Superimposed upon those diverse textures is the patina of Hesketh's use: stipple of paint-spatter, scrape of shoe, habitual hand-rest on easel, smooth seat of stool. The space has curved itself round her like a shell, new spiral chambers forming as she turned in her mother-of-pearl lining. It is full of wood-panel driftwood slices being made ready for her to paint, among a landslide of books, records, tools, brushes, paint-tubes and objects with no use which I can imagine. On an old counter-top on trestles, along the whole length of the window, are still life subjects set up with the sea as a backdrop: white dishes of shells, piles of pebbles, glass fishing-net weights in nests of dried weed, an old jug wearing a ship's name round its neck like a lopsided rosette. I stood staring at this row of paintings-to-be as though it was a window into Hesketh's art.

She gave me a small painting on a thick block of wood of a white shell, a model ship in a bottle, a mug full of wheat and cornflowers with its crackled face anciently inscribed *A Masque of Summer*. By some alchemy it blazes with the light of that joyful season. Hesketh gave it with a flourish. I took the painting and propped it on the bookcase in my bedroom, where it glows like a bright window as the rain stampedes back and forth across the roof.

Meredith

If I could send London to you in this envelope I would. Imagine sliding the river down into the folded letter (the low-tide smell, the glistening embankment) so that it fills the valley of paper, then the towers and spires and high bridges clip the top of the upper crease, the containing sky tucked safely across. It's all here still, waiting for you.

On a daily level the dust, grime, smog, accumulated debris, are indescribable of course, how not? You know about that. But yesterday morning when I walked to work, there had been rain, then watery sun, and every building blazed. Glory, glory, a heavenly city – even though it was only dull old Langham Place. I try to remember that it can be like this.

II

Crambo

When there are enough flowers I take them to the spring to float on the water just where it bubbles, so the flowers dance on the rill, a fountain of flower-heads. Sometimes I cover the surface with petals, so the pool's surface isn't water at all any more, it's colours. The spring comes up near the church, inside the church mound really, so when they made the wall they had to go round it, and they built a little low shelter over it, like a cave, I don't know why. It's square with deep lines bevelled between all the big even blocks of stone, and a domed lid inside and an open archway. Now there are ferns growing in all the crevices, the steps down are slippery, usually it's only one step but sometimes in dry weather there are two. All the old kettles with holes in and chipped enamel pots for people to get their water out are cluttered on the steps. From the ceiling little white grainy icicles have grown where the drips come down, I ate one once but it wasn't nice.

The water wells up from the bottom quite clear, the pebbles and little gravel stones and sandy spaces look brighter down through the water than they do if they sit out in the air, more intense. You can't see exactly the place it comes up, there isn't a hole in the ground like a well-head where a dark shaft goes deep down into the earth, there's just a rising-place. If you look carefully you can see a whorl in the white sand perhaps, a faint finger-mark, like water filtering away through sand only backwards, draining upwards. That must be why it's so clear. Before, it just ran away across the road to join the ditch going to the marsh, but now there's an iron pipe which takes it out past the pump on the green, in the ground. Sometimes you hear it booming to itself in the iron pipe underneath where the ford used to be. The pump doesn't work very well now, it's all rusted up and crusted with salt, nobody bothers with it.

If you go inside the spring's hood it's dark, but the light from the archway falls on the water brightly like a white lamp beam pointing. It smells of dank stone, sweet water, and under-the-earth, the old smell of soil and big worms. If you wait in there long enough you hear the drips falling, the water-voice quietly chirruping to itself as it does all the time, liquid hymns, just a song about rising there and flowing out, then suddenly sometimes it grumbles like a hungry stomach churning air, and does a great burp. It always makes me laugh when that happens, but I wait until I get outside.

My ma told me that when she was a girl, people used to come there to make wishes, throw in a coin, drink a palmful of water, wish. There aren't any coins in there now, other people picked them out. I never made a wish there before, hadn't anything to wish for, until Kezia, then I wished she might never leave, never go away from here. I put in one of those old coins, a small one, gold, with a picture of a woman like a water-person on one side of it, and the sand slowly swallowed it, drifted across grain by grain until it was gone.

I keep it all tidy in there, as well as doing the flowers. Once I met a hedgehog in there having a drink, I made it go out. There are no frogs, or newts even, the water moves too much, it doesn't have plants in it so they don't like it, but animals sometimes come if the ditch-water gets too brackish, and they want it fresh not salty. They can drink it outside easily, where the pipe gushes it out into the marsh. You can take the water as long as you don't make it dirty, it never runs out. I used to carry water to my ma from there when the weather was dry, enough to fill the copper, all her bottles, top up the water-butt if it needed it, all the water she wanted for the cottage. Luckily it rains a lot.

One afternoon I was along at the end of the beach by the cut and I saw people coming down from inland along the top of the ditch bank by the marsh side, soldiers with guns and big backpacks and a horse and cart. It isn't easy to get a cart along there, it's too narrow really and the grass is deep over booby-trap rabbit holes. They got nearly to the dunes though, and then they all sank down onto the ground and smoked cigarettes and made tea. I thought they were going to make a camp there, but after a long rest some of them came up onto the dunes and they paced out the ground and measured it out and stood about for a long time. After a while they began to dig a hole on one of the gravelly places, and some of them dug great trenches in the sand and filled sacks with it and they made walls out of the sandbags, so the beach was all scarred and rucked up. It was a mess. It took them nearly a week and they built a little grey hut without any windows and a tiny low door which faced inland along a tunnel. It had thick walls and it was ugly.

All of them went away, but I couldn't go inside, it would have killed me to look in there, to be enclosed like a shrimp in the rock. I hated it. I hated them for coming and trespassing and leaving their coffin here. I would have gone to tell Kezia once, and Hesketh, but I was frightened to go there any more since She tried to kill me. A few days later the soldiers came back with a great gun dragged on wheels in bits, and they set it up inside the hut with its snout out to seawards. They went off again, but left three of them behind. I watched them, night and day, I kept my eye on them. No one else came near them, they did nothing but take it in turns to sit up on top of the hut and look out. Sometimes they cooked things, sometimes they played cards, often they slept. One of them ran up and down the stretch of beach in front of the hut without his shirt on, one of them scribbled in a book whenever he was outside. I saw them when they went to the hole they'd made for their lavatory, I saw them bare when they washed, I smelt them on the wind. Sometimes one of them walked to the road inland and was gone all night, sometimes a cart brought them things, but they never all went away at once. I realised that they planned to stay on my island for ever.

I measure summer. When the swallows come they bring the beginning of it. Kezia told me they fly with the blue sky in their beaks, trailing it like a scarf behind them, but really it often rains as well after they come, they don't mind. The swallows are the start, and the bees, the bees cover the marsh as soon as the lavender comes out, you can hear the hum above the noise the waves make. Lizards don't come until later, high summer, sometimes not at all. It has to be hot for them to wake up, then they come out moving in little ticks, so it seems there's something wrong with your eyes when they turn their flat scaly heads in a jerky line not a smooth swing, tick tick tick. After they've basked in the sun they get pliant again, and quick, so you have to catch them early when they feel cool, like jelly, and you can get them by the middle, otherwise they can twist away, leave the tail twitching in your hand and scurry away all stumpy. It grows again though, but you can't eat tail, it isn't nice. I only want to look at them, see their scaly eyelids close upwards.

Once I heard bees in the big tree near the church. At first

I thought it was inside my head, I shook it and shook it and rolled on the ground, but nothing came out. When I did that when I was little my ma used to look down my ears, but there was never anything down there, not that she could see. After a bit I realised the noise was up in the tree, a great crowd of bees inhabiting all the spaces under the leaves, along the branches, right up to the tree's crown. I ran away then, in case they all stung Crambo at once, but they were just singing.

The honey isn't salty, even from sea bees, even when to make it they gather the lavender which grows from the salt-bitten marsh. I've tasted it, so sweet yet strong, with the crumbling wax compartments still in it, smelling of the bees' fur and their dark tongues. I've eaten it out of their nests, sticky hunks of bee-gold, sometimes they'll let you take a piece carefully, without stinging too much. Don't find it often.

I know it was early summer when the soldiers came because the bees were awake already, the swallows long arrived, but no lizards stirring. When I lay in the long grass watching I could hear them all, and see all the different kinds, small russet brindled bees, honey-bees they are, workers, mad bees with an orange hump back, larger ones with white bums, or striped half and half instead of more thinner stripes, the big bumbles which live in holes like birds in the sandbanks, small angry ones with dangling forelegs, the silvery-white ones like ancient bees gone ghostly grey. They were all out there, not knowing anything was different.

Fitz

Hesketh called us up to the studio; she said the seals were giving a synchronised swimming display. We perched on easel-stools up at the window drinking coffee, taking it in turns to look through Benbow, pointing out to each other where the seals' serious dog-like faces poked up through the wave-shadows. I have never seen seals before except at the zoo; I found their human way of swimming surprising and touching. It was a bright hopeful morning, a sea-change in the air, one's dreams not so wildly impossible. We were there in a laughing row, delicately cheerful, when straight across the front of our view came a soldier running. He jogged along the sea margin, picking up his feet, puffing like the parody of a trainee runner: chest out, shoulders back, fists up, neat heels. Hesketh frowned, perhaps wondering if this was an illusion; Kezia looked as though she might dissolve into a sea mist.

'Where did he spring from?' (I spoke first.)

'The cataclysm has reached even here,' Hesketh said wearily. 'The dust blows everywhere.'

Some strange polite constraint prevented me from asking if this was really the first such intrusion into their enclosed world. But how did the beach escape a full-scale anti-invasion barricade years ago, when everyone believed that an enemy landing was imminent? And if not then, why now? I almost feel as though I've broken their spell of invisibility just by being here.

Since then we have seen the soldiers often. We can hear singing when the wind is in the right direction, or sometimes just a kind of drunken bellowing not unlike Crambo's serenades. Hesketh treats their presence with a mocking kind of disdain, once remarking to me that they seem like very young boys to be out on their own so late at night. But Kezia resents their presence, is afraid of them yet determined to ignore them. She never walks in that direction alone, always turns back to the house if she sees one of them in the distance; her small world has shrunk still further. It made her tell me about Crambo, though.

'He was my friend,' she said, stirring the soup urgently. 'When I was little we played together all the time. He was a bit odd – I suppose – but I didn't really notice – he was so clever. I still have lots of things he made for me – wonderful things he found. We were able to talk together quite well then – I could understand him better – he learnt to talk much more – and read...'

'You taught him to read?' I exclaimed.

'Just his name – things like that – he isn't wrong in the head, you know – it was only that his mother couldn't manage and she didn't get any help – he never went to school.'

After I had acknowledged that Crambo was not a monster of any kind, she related the rest of the rather inevitable tale. He gradually descended into a sort of madness she could not understand; their hand-holding, sand-wrestling, basking in the shallows, strolling in the dunes, became oddly distasteful to her. He scrabbled and snatched at her, stared too intensely, touched too insistently, until she became gradually more withdrawn. One morning when she was alone in a hollow bowl of the grass, reading, he pounced. Skinny though he is, he must be strong. She fought him off (she must have a dangerous temper like her mother, I thought, watching her eyes glitter at the thought of it). As they were rolling about in this hideous pseudo-embrace, Hesketh appeared. She stood silhouetted on the brow of the hillock, looking impassively down the sights of the raised rifle she was holding, straight at Crambo. (I can just see that.) He screamed like a ferret-struck rabbit, shrill and high, and ran off; he must have seen animals shot before.

'How did she know?' I asked uneasily.

Kezia shrugged.

'She just knew.'

This is another example of what I don't understand here. Crambo has been punished by his separation from Kezia, his fear of Hesketh, but that is all. Does he understand, or even remember why? They appear not to hold his actions against him, any more than they could blame a hungry lion for trying to eat someone – though they note that it is not safe to give it the chance. Is this saintly, or merely pragmatic? I cannot tell what they think, how they think, at all.

Uncannily, Hesketh appeared at my moment of need too, just before the soldiers came. It hadn't occurred to me that it might be possible to get lost in Saltstreet, with the constant reference points of the sea, the horizon, the dunes, the inland hills, immovable markers. No compass error could confuse the wanderer's whereabouts on such a map, its grid so visibly marked … or so I thought. But when I was on the beach alone, out on the tide-flat, I saw a tall white wave out towards the horizon, a fold on the margin; it rolled in like the moving wall of water which a spring tide might raise, but it was mist. It advanced faster than the sea, so solid-seeming that as it approached me I felt an impulse to flee from it, perhaps even took a few steps back before it overtook me. Within its sudden shroud was silence, but for distorted noises, a contrasting chill, absolute fog-blindness. No cloth dropped over a parrot could cut off all points of contact so completely, impose such utter isolation.

In London, certainly, fogs are common enough; those

smog-laden 'particulars' so beloved of shocker writers, in which people can't see the proverbial hand before their faces. I've often walked home guiding myself by the railings, crossed roads arm-in-arm with stumbling strangers, heard policemen standing on corners calling out the street name. I have driven along the kerb-side as slowly as the car's engine could bear, while my erstwhile passenger walked at the pavement edge to guide me. But this sea fog was different. Instead of voices, laughter, curses, grinding engines, or patches of dim street lamp or headlight to inhabit the mist, there was nothing, a void. No noise I could recognise reached through the whiteness, its milk-in-water swirls formed shapes which the imagination read as figures looming up close then suddenly dissolving. Black spots began to drift across the blank screen onto which my vision could not resist projecting something. I stooped down to make out my footprints, to return the way I had come, but the damp sand-slick had not held them.

Before I'd gone more than a few yards, I thought I could hear the sea in front of me, a distant hiss which might almost be footsteps rushing on gravel, instead of waves. I listened in both directions, but the mist seemed to create some echo effect; the sound was all around me. I took out my watch to check the time, but it had stopped. The curlicues, blocks of sea cloud, grey shadow patches, still formed themselves into elaborate shapes, towered over me, danced at the edges of my sight, disintegrated. Several times I stopped dead, convinced I was about to dash myself against a barrier which, when I put my hands out cautiously, proved an illusion. My foot sent a stone spinning into a shard of driftwood; its eerie clattering sound startled me. I drove the wood upright into the sand as a way-marker, to test out my suspicion that I might be walking round in circles. Some time later I passed (or rather almost tripped over) a piece of wood which was extremely similar – the same one fallen over, perhaps. The paleness of the mist, which had so tantalisingly suggested it might be half-transparent, became less ghostly, less tiring to the eyes, less opaline. I realised it was indeed getting dark.

This was the moment when I called out, a desolate greeting which received no answer. I felt foolish, shouting hellos to myself on the beach, an English embarrassment at my own existence. I called Hesketh, Kezia, Crambo by their names in case they could hear me, but no one answered. The lie of the land gave no sign of where I was, and even if I had known the beach better, could read its landmarks, its different stretches of sand or stone, I doubt I could have seen enough in that blindfold to be sure that I recognised where I was. I decided to stand still, wait for it to clear, hang around as though waiting for a rare late bus that was bound to come along in the end. A black dog shot past, almost cannoned into me; the fog was so thick that I only glimpsed it for a second when it nearly touched me, then doubted I'd really seen it. I shouted again in case it had an owner, but there was no reply.

There was a moment out there on the sand flats when I felt more terror than being lost could really warrant. I was not afraid of the incoming tide, of staying out all night, of falling in the creek, but simply of being alone in that abysmal place. I thought that all my training, my ability to endure cold or hunger, blitz or boredom, had not prepared me for anything at all.

Another figure came towards me through the fog, wavering dark against the less dark, and did not dissolve. The hair stood up on my neck for a moment, it seemed such a tall dour thing, then I saw.

'Hesketh!'

'Here I am.' She touched my shoulders.

'What a relief! I thought I might be out here all night.'

She smiled, so far as I could see, spun me round, gave me a little push in the small of the back.

'Go on, straight up there, home. You can't miss it. I'll be back in a moment.'

Obediently, I went. Soon I recognised the tideline, the slope up towards the dunes, the shallow terraces which turned into the stepped path up to the boathouse. In barely five minutes I was back. Kezia gave me a cup of tea, exclaimed with concern that I'd been caught by a summer sea mist, suggested a game of chess. I was delighted as any sailor to be home, even that 'home' which is only our hotel room in a foreign city, our berth on the overnight train. At her usual time, Hesketh descended from the studio for her bath.

Poor Kezia must find me a dull companion. I try to befriend her, but I've more in common with Hesketh; in front of Kezia I always feel I should watch my language, curb my spirits. With Hesketh it's different; she has a worldly-bohemian air which puts me at my ease. I can imagine her in a little restaurant in Soho, or up in the gods at the theatre; with Kezia such a scene is hard to frame. She is by no means ethereal – she's a practical countrywoman who works hard, but she remains otherworldly, untouchable. Although she wants my companionship, she stays at a distance. Now that my letter has arrived to summon me for a medical review, I thought she might like to come along for the outing. (It's only as far as the county town, a dull journey by bus and train, but possible to return within the day.) To my relief, she refused instantly with something like panic.

That same afternoon, yesterday perhaps, it was fine. The

tide came slowly in over its miles of warm sand; for the first time I saw the water clear, the sun casting its net of light down through the shallows, reflections flying on the sand beneath. I rolled up my trousers to wade with bare feet meshed in sunlight. It was strange, delightful, to be able to walk out so far that the sea extended on all sides, but was not yet knee-deep. Kezia paddled beside me, continually pointing out water-creatures around our toes, miniature crabs and shrimps and darting fish. She took my arm (her hand so light it hardly weighed through my shirt sleeve); from the far shore behind us, I heard Crambo's desolate, distant shout.

Kezia

Fitz told me once that seagulls reminded her of home. I was surprised – until she described them in flocks on the river – pursuing the barges – lining the bridge-edges. Then I heard their raucous screaming as a city-sound. We watched one of them dropping a sealed shell from the height where it hovered – repeatedly diving to find the clam – or whatever it was – still unbroken.

'You'll have to drop it on a stone, mate,' Fitz called to the gull. 'It's not going to work on the sand, is it?' To me she added 'Daft thing' more quietly – as though not to hurt its feelings.

The bird continued its efforts – unavailing – until on one fluke attempt we heard the distinct crack of the shell opening – saw the gull plunge triumphantly to its meal. I told Fitz about the long-beaked waders that either drill through the shells – or twist them open – but never use both methods – their beaks show which. She remarked that people were just the same – but wouldn't elaborate. She relapsed into her usual silence after this – but when I took her arm she smiled at me – obligingly moved her cigarette over to the other hand – gave me her attention.

It wasn't just cracked courtesy (I thought) which made Fitz speak to seagulls – bow to herons – stand up when Hesketh came into the room – walk arm-in-arm with me on a sunless afternoon when she would no doubt have preferred to be reading. Fitz was – I asked Hesketh what the quality was – she said 'hearts of oak' – a compliment we often assigned to faithful dogs, returning sailors or other minor folk-heroes. I was amused to recognise – after that – one of Fitz's few whistling-tunes was *Come cheer up my lads 'tis to glory we steer* – they only ever lasted one phrase. The other snatches were – *We'll keep the red flag flying* – *None but the brave deserve the fair* – *London Pride*, inevitably – just those – in rotations which may have been indicative of mood – or merely random. It did not surprise me – then – that Hesketh never seemed irritated by Fitz's presence – did not resent this invasion of our long privacy – although she certainly made no allowances for the presence of a stranger – didn't treat Fitz as a guest who needed entertaining – kept to her usual patterns of work or sleep – she actually seemed to like talking to her, sometimes. I listened to them like a child eavesdropping on adult conversations – intrigued – sometimes mystified – slightly impatient. Once – after they'd had a long discussion about whether making cakes for one's friends was indeed a lower note sounded within the same creative scale as writing music like Mozart – a premise which Fitz had read in one of her great tomes – I asked Hesketh if she thought Fitz would always be our friend. She answered absently, 'Oh, we'll never lose her.'

It was difficult to explain to Fitz about Crambo. One day we were lounging on the sand-scoop armchairs just below the house – a sunbath with gloves on, as she said – while she stared up at the sky as intently as she must have at the cinema screen before – her arms folded behind her head. Over us – in a dark symmetrical cloud – flew a formation of planes passing as slowly as the geese flocks – drowning the sea's steady singing with a louder blustering drone – all the raging engines in a conspiracy. After they had passed the silence still seemed vibrant with aftershock.

'Do you think the world is going to end?' she said quietly.

'I suppose so.'

In the distance I could hear Crambo bewailing – his fear

– the planes' inexplicable passage.

Our first meeting – as children – promised better than the awkward situation we had come to. Exploring outside – early days – I saw a figure in the distance – a black beetle silhouette on the pale dunes – which appeared comically over each hill brow and vanished again as it ran down the slope into the hollow between. Through Benbow I could see it was weirdly clothed in many layers of tattered shirts and scarves which flailed about impeding its fast, crab-like progress. Closer, the waving antennae were strange protuberances – curved sticks and bones – attached to a top hat encrusted with limpet shells. I could not decide if the tanned – smooth – *blank* – face was an older boy or a boylike man – it wasn't like any face I knew. I thought the yodelling noises with waving arms were in greeting, but when he reached me he gave a yelp of surprise and lurched on. It was a long time before he became (I thought) my friend. And then not my friend again.

Fitz was sick of him. She had begun to echo his speechlessness – gave a low growl at the sound of him – a grunt of irritation when he appeared. But she was not unkind.

'Could he hear the bombers?' she asked.

'Yes, and I think he can feel them as well, more than we do. The disturbance in the air. And he knows what they are, somehow.'

'Poor fellow. No wonder he's scared.'

I had a terrible feeling that Fitz might be about to ask me why I hadn't been conscripted – at my age – or at least had to do some war work – so I quickly questioned her as I never did about herself, her own war. She just laughed, rather mirthlessly.

'I joined up early on, to fight Fascism; as you know I'm a Red – pinko, anyway. I had my own reasons for wanting to, as well, but not very good reasons. I wanted to wear trousers to work, to be heroic. That seems a long time ago now. I was brought up a pacifist, too – sometimes I think I'd have done better to stick to that, the lost ideal, but it didn't seem possible, not with what they were doing to people of my kind. Whether my contribution has been invaluable is an open question, I'm afraid – I do know a lot about the combustion engine, though.'

I didn't know what she meant – I said so. Fitz grinned.

'I just mean I've spent a lot of time driving people about, then for the last few years driving one important person about so well that I got promoted – hardly the work of heroes. I might have done better, taken a more honourable course. There have to be some people who dissent, some who carry on work in the libraries while the barbarians scale the frontier walls.'

'Like Hesketh?'

Fitz looked rather surprised – but she agreed.

'Your ma, the BBC, Shakespeare – we've won the battle of culture anyway. They've only got Wagner...'

(I knew now when she was joking.)

As Crambo reached another crescendo Fitz suddenly roared 'Oh, *shut up*' – then, seeing my face, added more gently – 'Kezia, he can't hear me.'

The pollution of the shore – the desecration – gradually increased. Barbed wire spread along – rubbish caught and fluttered on it. I had never really believed that any invader would land on our quiet coast – but now I listened uneasily for the church bells – wondered if it would be wise to have a wireless – did not admit that these aliens who had come seemed the same to me as any others. Fitz bracingly told me that our forces had landed in France, not the other way round, it was no secret; these oafs were belatedly here because of some mad theory or rumour, but if we were in any real danger we would all have been evacuated. I didn't believe her. (I felt we were in more danger now.) No one would try to move Hesketh. They'd come more than once to talk to her about something like that – requisitioning, billeting, evacuating, jargon words for forcing – she charmed them away. I heard them say when they came again, 'Oh she's the poor little mad girl' – about me. Once a mangled brown envelope came – addressed to me – my name as I never gave it. I passed the paper to Hesketh – she held it at arm's length to read – looked at me with a little downturned-mouth grimace – said, 'I'll have to write to them again.' Nothing else happened. Fitz never asked me the questions I dreaded – she was not an asker of awkward ones – not an opener of cupboard doors which she heard rattling – perhaps she presumed I had some official exemption – or perhaps she didn't perceive me as a possible war-worker. We were invisible – forgotten – beyond the margin.

Fitz's presence perhaps made things seem different. When she wanted to go exploring, I told her that the only society for miles about was at the pub by the quay in Saltstreet village where women went rarely and never alone. Gentry were represented by the big house some miles inland with a fabled old owner who never came out. There must have been – further along the coast – a school and a shop and a post office – but not that I knew about. As far as I was aware local spirits of place brought us our post – our deliveries – parcels from Hesketh's wine merchant or library – sometimes I waved to their faraway figures – but Fitz expected to meet them. She was on weather-remarking terms with people I had never heard of as soon as she could reach the coast road, *hail-fellow-well-met* camaraderie dissipating her strangeness. I thought that if she encountered one of the soldiers, she would probably speak even to him.

We had more sunny days – her stride lengthened – she would be going back to London soon – after her medical – leaving us with our armed guard. I acknowledged that I had been looking forward to showing her the place in summer – relying on her company. Now when she was silent I would try to draw her out – ask her questions about London – about her time at the University – the job she had started just when the war began – her childhood house which was bombed – the room she'd rented in her friend's flat in a newish block on the Gray's Inn Road. There was little detail about any of this – she never talked about her family except when mentioning something she did as a child. I thought perhaps they'd been killed in the blitz. Once she got out a street map of London and showed me how to walk through from there to the British Museum or down to the West End and the river.

'Mecklenburgh Square got it,' she said then. 'All those garden squares have lost one side or more. But that flat's still there. Jocelyn says it's too hideous to go.'

We looked out across the marsh, flooded by high spring tides into a still expanse of mirror water reflecting the sheet of white sky. I didn't ask whether she would prefer to stay in this place – still a sanctuary, however defiled – because I knew that for some reason I could not understand, she wanted nothing but to go back.

The everyday beauties of the place only seemed to exacerbate her homesickness. Clouds – the entire pink-freckled sky which so exactly imitated the wave-stippled sand beneath – the wild pale banners streaming above us in saltires or slashes – the dark violet broiling layers of cloud-clod breaking open to spill out scarlet sunset – the white high-piled froth constantly dissolving and refoaming itself as it passed – all reminded her of the open skies over the Heath. Stars – which we saw with a vivid magnificence uninterrupted by any glare from the ground – made her speak of the sight of Orion rising diagonal behind chimneys as the first sign of autumn. Yet, when I saw her stargazing – pointing out a shooting star for me to wish on – or asking if I thought a certain constellation could yet be hoist over our low horizon – I thought she was even coming to be fond of the place – in her way – as she surely was of Hesketh – and me too – but that she could only see it as a make-believe land – no more than half-real – a dusk in which her dream must be endured until morning – daylight – awakening.

A note came – Fitz said it had been 'shoved under the door'. It said:

On my walks along the beach I'm sometimes privileged to meet a barefoot princess, or perhaps she is a mermaid, who has stolen my heart. I think she is shy because when I try and speak to her, she vanishes like a moonbeam. I hope one day she will relent.

It was signed with various military titles and numbers – like a prisoner.

I showed it to Fitz, between crab-pincer finger and thumb. (Hesketh was in the studio already.)

Fitz grunted, 'I expect he says that to all the girls.'

I could not laugh. I glowered at her – cracked my knuckle joints – snorted. She put her arm round my shoulders in that rough-gentle way which I found so oddly comforting – and squeezed.

'He must need specs.'

'It's hateful.'

'It's just daft.'

Fitz continued to be – no other word for it – brotherly, but I had a feeling she understood my dumb fury.

Princess, forsooth! Mermaid, maybe. There are powerful mermaids – mermaids with siren voices to sink ships and call up storms – mermaids who are quite the opposite of princesses – whose bodies are naked out of choice, for their own convenience – who live outside the conventions of land life – who are risky to speak to, dangerous to meet. Mermaids with breasts. But I knew he meant the sort of mermaid who is helpless – can't walk – has to be carried about – has no interests but hairdressing and jewellery – and even in these suitably feminine pursuits is childishly simple, content with hair-combing and shell-collecting.

Worst of all – to be perceived like this – was it my own fault? I couldn't help being small – slight – wary – but it was perhaps culpable to have such long hair – seem shy – and move, in that detestable phrase, like a moonbeam. Nobody (I thought) would dream of writing such rot to a woman like Hesketh – a proper woman with that solid quality of magnificence – the sort of woman who had, as I heard Fitz say once when she was talking about some actress, 'a touch of the Goddess'. I fleetingly imagined being transformed into a woman like that – the sort of woman Fitz apparently admired – rather than the sort that appealed to the unknown soldier. Age would help – this had not occurred to me before – but so would going to London to buy a black evening dress – have my hair expensively set and possibly dyed – my face and nails, even toenails, professionally painted. Since none of this was remotely possible – for so many reasons – I found the kitchen scissors to snip off Rapunzel.

With perseverance, I was able to cut my hair quite short – even with the enormous steel scissors, on my own. The hair looked several shades darker – more like Hesketh's – it began to curl slightly. Unfortunately, the effect was gamine – I had no idea whether I looked older – too old for long hair – or like a ten-year-old. But at least – as I said to Fitz – I'd prefer to look like a tinker's brat – a hard-to-catch guttersnipe poaching on the foreshore – than fucking Tinkerbell. I boiled with rage when I thought of running on the beach – turning cartwheels – flying my kite – before they came, or Crambo changed – when I had to walk like a veiled woman, wearing Hesketh's long macintosh to cover my shorts.

Fitz and Hesketh were both very nice about my hair – assured me that it suited me so often that I had to suspect it did not. It made them feel a bit sad (I think) – the end of Rapunzel – especially Hesketh. But it was too late then, it had gone. I took to wearing a handkerchief knotted over my head – an old check one – which – with the long macintosh and bare feet – made me look like a fishwife out to pick illicit cockles. It was not princess-like.

Meredith

You will have read, even in your isolation, or perhaps heard (if you can listen in to the wireless while marooned on your desert island) how things are here. Even by day the flying bombs drone over, the walls fall down, people listen to the sky again. It is, we are assured, the last gasp of a defeated enemy, a final act of vengeance on our indestructible city. Beneath all the patriotic rhetoric I think this holds some golden fragments of truth, when all the sand and river mud is sieved out. Even in the midst of the devastation there's that sense that we survive, oddly undiminished; even the incessant complaining is surely an obstinate wish for things to be as they were. Never the same again, or all the same in a hundred years? Both accurate, perhaps.

Once, during those early years of war when we still expected to be able to go out in the evening and presumed we'd get home, I was walking back after a late shift at work, when a raid started. It was a summer night, not warm but mild, all gold and blue; the searchlights stroking the sky above the trees were reflected in their leaves, pale against the indistinct blue houses beyond. I saw a tall woman ahead of me, a grey silhouette, not hurrying on but standing in the middle of the street with her arms raised to the sky, laughing. As the planes came closer, I stepped into the portico of one of those stucco houses with a wide door; I called to her to come up to the shelter of the porch with me, but of course she couldn't hear. She walked on, with a curious swaying walk, half-dance, with many pauses. Occasionally she spun slowly round, arms lifted again. Then she disappeared into the distances of the square, quite unharmed, while the shrapnel and debris fell round her like fiery rain.

During raids I often think of her, like a talisman, a figure made visible by that extreme disruption of the atmosphere – the genius of a place, perhaps some London square – unscathed, amused, crazed. I suppose she was just a woman going home after dinner, drunkenly elated, rather than a sad wild spirit carolling, 'Lord, what fools these mortals be.' I hope she got back safe, with the immunity of the innocent; I expect so. But I like to imagine that other elemental vision, dancing with the darkness, ecstatic and unafraid, defying all destruction. It's a weird comfort to me – a sight that matched this unlikely time.

Fitz

Crambo is an unacceptable monster (only think of his table manners) but sometimes I envy him the freedom to roar out his anger, frustration or delight. I'm a more acceptable one, but still his kin under the clothes, my part-convincing disguise. Why Hesketh summoned me here I'm still none the wiser, really. Did she hope for a rescuer? When she sent for a convalescent officer did she imagine a stranger who would resolve their situation? If so, I'm unsuitable for the role for several reasons. Kezia would never let herself be carried off into the sunset, anyway: she's too firmly fixed here while the world crumbles round us.

We woke up one morning, and the way to the sea was barred, we were corralled in the dunes by those undulating springs of barbed wire so familiar from the older wars. Presently a soldier came to the door with a clumsily typed notice that the beach was out-of-bounds to civilians; it was going to be mined. We would no longer be able to walk down to the water without danger of death. Hesketh dealt with him mockingly, distantly. She didn't bother to ask, why now? I suddenly wondered if she and Kezia thought of me as 'one of them' also, to be mollified, impressed, then privately cursed. In the town I heard that in some villages, out-of-the-way places where no one ever went, they threw stones at the soldiers, telling them to go away in accents so broad as to be hardly understood. It wasn't that the villagers mistook them for the enemy army, but they were foreign enough, being from away, to need chasing off.

Curiously, my medical trip to the market town has made me feel more of a stranger, an outsider, to my hosts; it reminded me that I am a cog in an infernal machine (which is still paying me). My impersonation of a disciplined efficient worker has become so good that sometimes I am taken in by it myself, almost forget my deeper allegiances. This phenomenon, which I've heard called over-identification with the role, doesn't last long. Soon the ordinary casual outlaw reappears, slightly sheepish at such convincing collaboration with the other side. For I can no longer believe that my so-called work has made any difference to anything; I might as well have spent the last five years like many people I know, wearing elaborate uniforms to chat self-importantly in restaurants, or making the propaganda which assures people like me that our contribution has been crucial. Any desire for heroism has long been purged by boredom, routine, witness of random violence. I can't doubt that I would have been a better warrior by practising my small art. As it is, I have nothing to be proud of. It was only by luck that I escaped the darker duties.

And it all comes back to me, quite easily, the memory of the time immediately before the thing happened. I was driving back into London one evening, as fast as I dared in the semi-darkness, looking forward to a bath and a drink. It was clear, almost frosty. I'd dropped the boss off for the weekend; I was free until Sunday evening. As I crossed Waterloo bridge I could see the river sinuously reflecting the white sky, the moon standing beside Big Ben's dark tower like a double for the unlit clock-face. It was so still that the throbbing of the siren as it began seemed an insane interruption. St Paul's glimmered above the water like a beautiful illusion, an elaborate painted stage set. I reckoned there was time to get away from the river, back to the safety of our garages; it was a difficult car but I was fond of it.

I was just turning northwards when I saw two women scurrying along the pavement on the other side of the road.

One of them was old and couldn't keep up; her companion (perhaps her daughter?) was trying to hurry her along, but tenderly. I knew they must be making for a shelter, but without much chance of getting in if they didn't make it quick, so I pulled over, called to them to jump in for a ride. I drove through the squares towards the tube, with the siren still incessantly moaning, while they told me I ought to get a medal – such nice women, keeping up a good front for each other in that fear-contaminated atmosphere. The younger one wished me all the luck in the world, even as they dived down into the station.

I sped off before anyone could interfere, but – as I turned up my side-street shortcut towards the mews – there was the unmistakable gigantic whine of one of those evil devices as it fell, the annihilating violence of its impact, the vast gasp of all the air moving in a block, expelled to somewhere else. The car flipped over sideways, propelled I suppose by this invisible wind, then skidded fast along the pavement, pursued by the wave of the falling building which rippled into a brick drift around and over everything. Some dangling railings brought the car to a neat stop, just beyond the tide-line, parked.

All ended; I thought that was it, over. I realised that it wasn't. I could see stars through tree-branches as the choking fog cleared; I even thought I heard a blackbird singing. My hand was crushed under me; when I tried to move it, I fainted. If I'd left the car to go back towards the shelter I'd have been under the building. People said it had been a late warning, but such complaints are commonplace. I woke up in the hospital, still caked with old dust, doubtless stinking, strangely exalted. (Meredith came to see me, unless I dreamt that – she brought violets.) All the rest I had never forgotten.

It makes a difference somehow, the remembering, even the fear and the blast as well as the stars and the blackbird. My everyday life seems more real to me, more noticeably confined, but this amnesiac diary ceases to obsess me. I write sometimes to Meredith. She asked for tales of my life here; what can I tell her, except that in the evenings I light the oil lamps for the house, in the morning clean them and fill them, carry logs, pump water, feed the Rayburn. News have I none. I described some of Crambo's strange dwellings or decorations in the dunes; totem poles of old boots and anchovy tins; boats outlined in the ground like buried ships emerging from a mound, where he evidently lies sometimes, going on unknown voyages; sheaves of reeds set like standing stones in a dancers' circle; net curtains encrusted with colour-themed scraps of purplish weed, purple-tinged shell, purple-veined rock, purple lettered tin in pride of place, sea lavender flowers garlanded all around. I think she will like this, be interested, be able to see it.

Also I told her that I begin, hesitantly at first but with increasing flow, to think about my work again (my proper work), to collect the things I need to make the whole box of tricks, to sketch out, imagine, conceive. Possibly I have Crambo to thank for this slight stirring of creative sap – has he put me to shame by his unceasing making? It may not come to anything, anyway.

Kezia makes me go everywhere with her now because the soldiers, unable to exercise on the beach, come along the dunes instead, right past the front of the house, sometimes stop. Hesketh has cautioned Kezia not to be rude to them, so she is mute. It's always the same crew; they never appear to have reinforcements or go off duty. The one who wrote to her, Dominic Stevens, seems a harmless enough bookish young man. He has got her name somehow, will occasionally approach, murmur it to her like a charm. Unfortunately, her name is a ludicrous indicator of accent, from Crambo's rough *Kesh-ar* to Stevens' more proper *Kays-yer,* rhyming with hazier. (I would have Kezia rhyme with desire...)

As her resigned escort yesterday, I lay on my back in the dunes, cushioned on sand which rasped on my shirt, staring at the sky so I didn't have to see the barbed wire nest we were cosied down in. Beside me, Kezia was seated rather primly, arms clasped round drawn-up knees, chin angled skywards. Larks were calling from very high above us.

'Look,' she said. 'A seal.'

Almost level with us, quite close in to the mined beach, the dark head sleekly broke the sea's surface, vanished for a long moment, reappeared somewhere unexpected with a conjurer's smug air. It gave me the same pain round the heart that Kezia did, the tender anxiety for its innocence, the fear that it did not understand how things really are. Suddenly it raised its shoulders up out of the water to float upright, examining us with urbane curiosity, snorting gently to itself. I loved it; laughing inwardly I recognised that its wisdom was far superior to mine (and that also was like Kezia).

'One of your relatives,' I said, pointing to it.

Kezia stood rigidly, staring, hands clenched, the wind plastering her mac to her skinny knees.

'I'm going to speak to her.'

'Let's wave. She can see us.'

We waved, Kezia with fluttering hands to a royal train flashing by, I with the wide sweeping arcs of a castaway attracting rescuers. The seal regarded us gravely, its dark liquid prima-donna eyes bulging slightly.

'I must go to her.'

Before I could hold her she was off, running as though someone was shooting at her, dodging in and out of the barbed wire tendrils, an incongruous phantom in no-man's land. I roared, forgetting our neighbours in their blockhouse, our pact of silence and separateness.

'Kezia, no! Come back!'

She plunged down out of my sight for a moment, reappeared on the harder damped-down beach sand below the tideline. Lightly she ran across it, almost danced, with weaving steps until she halted at the water's very edge, where the ripple ends that was once a wave. The seal turned a slow back somersault, disappeared without trace back into its own opaque domain. Kezia wandered along the wave-side, picking up shells, squatting down to examine the sea's offerings. There was no geyser of mud and water, no subaqueous explosion. I realised when I tasted the blood in my mouth that I'd bitten the insides of my cheeks into furrows.

Kezia came running back, thumped herself down on the slope beside me, a little breathless. I was locked so rigid against my trembling that I could not move.

'I think she recognised me. She raised her flippers like wings – like an angel.'

'Kezia, are you mad? Have you forgotten about the mine-field?'

'There aren't many along here. I know more or less where they are.'

'*More or less?* Do you know what those things do if they detonate?'

'Crambo runs about on the beach all the time.'

'*Crambo!*' I exclaimed furiously. 'He would.'

'He's never set one off – he knows where they are. There are paths between them now.'

'They're not fucking fireworks that you can "set off", and you're not the village idiot to behave like that. What would Hesketh do if you had your foot blown off?'

'You're hurting my arm, Fitz.'

I let go abruptly, turned away from her to trudge back to the house. It occurred to me that Kezia (walking impenitently behind me) probably often flitted across the surface of the sand like a long-legged insect on a puddle, making no indentation on the tender surface, trusting to the water-skin to keep dry footed. It made the sweat break out on my temples to think of it. As we returned to our claustrophobic safety she slipped her arm through mine, said lightly 'Don't be angry'.

Kezia

When Fitz had gone off – very early – to have her medical, I went into her room to get a book. I thought I ought to get on with something – I wanted the star book, so that I could do some more astronomy to help with my navigation. The room wasn't very tidy – although it was clean enough – maybe a bit dusty – it smelt of Fitz's scent – cologne? – her sweet cinnamony tobacco. There was a charming photo which I knew was her with her mother – the smiling woman rather prettily plump and elegant – the child chivalrously attentive. Beside it – also in a frame – was a colour postcard of a large foreign hotel – all balconies and little café tables. There were two letters on the washstand, which I read. One – which started *My Dear* – was from someone called Meredith – quite short but indefinably intimate. I read it – snorted – read again. The other was more formal – typed – something to do with permission to repair a damaged house – puzzlingly addressed to 'F. L. Fitzroy Esq.'

I went into Hesketh's studio, where she was on the divan with her feet up, drinking sherry.

'Do you know anything about Fitz's bombed house?' I asked.

'Oh, yes, poor Fitz, I don't think she likes to talk about it much, but she told me that it's very small, a cottage almost, in a lane somewhere up by Parliament Hill – that's northwards, near the Heath. Rather too close to the railway for its own good, just the shell left. I suppose it may be reparable – but it's shaken her, hasn't it?'

'There wasn't anybody in there when it happened?'

'No, no. She just came back from work one day to find it like that. Not a direct hit, as they please to call it, just collateral damage.'

'So do you know what's happened to her family? Has she told you anything?'

Hesketh was silent – looked at me – her always liquid eyes welled full.

'She's lost her mother, literally. The poor woman was caught on the continent when war broke out, and Fitz has had no word for a long time now. But of course all may yet be well – she should hear something soon. No father in evidence. Her grandfather was wounded in Spain, seven years ago – then he died not long after. So she's alone. She said that her work had kept her going, at the beginning.'

'And what is her work?'

'Well, I think she must be in Intelligence, don't you?' Hesketh suggested more cheerfully. 'Awfully bright, speaks lots of languages, rather odd, just the type. Everything terribly mysterious, and rather high-ranking to be just a driver. Codes, I expect. Everyone knows that all that crew are spies. I think that must be what her mother was doing abroad.'

'What about Meredith?'

'No, don't know,' Hesketh said, but I was sure she did. (She was a terribly bad liar – too brazen.) 'Now I must get on, while the light lasts.'

I wandered off – pondering that this was as much as I knew about my own forbears – celandine anecdotes gleaming out of dim undergrowth. Careful questions arising from these stories – 'Why did they call your mother *Madam* Hesketh?' – produced enthusiastic answers not exactly to the purpose. 'Oh, it's just a courtesy title, darling; in Scotland they still say "Mistress" too sometimes, not only to the Laird's lady. I suppose it's to do with the Auld Alliance – we christened a wonderful cocktail by that name in Paris; champagne for

France and a whisky liqueur for Scotland...' – she was off – leaving me little the wiser.

Fitz got back very late – brought to the end of the causeway (she said) by a Red Cross supply truck taking chocolate to the coastal defences. She had been rated still unfit to return to duty but it would not be long now – there was some other job she might be able to do until she could drive again – she was so excited I could hardly understand what she was saying – it was all acronym or nickname. There had even been talk about what would happen at eventual demobilisation, the distant end of the war. She kept saying, 'I'd still be in London, London-based...' The hand which had been injured – her left – shook as she held her cigarette in it – she impatiently flexed it – clenched it – it would almost make a fist now. When I stood up – went to boil the water for the bottles – she gave me a comradely grin. As I carried my scalding load upstairs I heard Hesketh ask warmly 'Did you manage to telephone?' and Fitz's voice dipped hoarsely as she answered.

I understood – too suddenly – why people stay in their houses when the sea is eating away the cliffs – the burial ground goes – the stone crosses and headstones slump downhill – other closer houses crash ruinously into the water – but they hang on – unable to relinquish their title to that immutable place – home. Unless they have upsticks moved – flung the cooking pots back in the caravan, whistled up the dogs, harnessed the old horse – it's too hard. They may feel that there is some invisible bulwark – which protects them as it did not the others – or perhaps their powers of self-preservation are paralysed by the implausibility of the danger. It wasn't until the war brought itself to our doorstep that I realised what our situation was – had been all along. We had moved out beyond the pale by our own choice – now we squatted in a condemned building – unsuitable for human habitation – beyond the reach of safety regulations or standards – no one's responsibility but our own. Hesketh asked if I wanted to leave now that the soldiers had come – I said no. There were too many reasons – for us as for everyone always – why we couldn't leave our home – not then – not yet. It was something we would get used to – grow round and overflow – like a tree with wire embedded in its body. I would prefer to stay there – even in some deformed shape – than ever leave, ever go away.

Hesketh assured me that it was perfectly safe – she was our bulwark – nothing bad could happen – no harm would come to us. I believed her. Fitz too was a companion who could help keep the beach safe – a good ally – and so on. We would hold out – not let ourselves be disturbed – it would pass – surely. When does the moment come when we admit something is spoilt? The new road has come too near – the factory smoke means we cannot breathe – the noise is now unendurable. But let us hold out – like the people on the cliff edge – only in the very last seconds do they scrabble to safety – if it is not already too late – the impossible now in the process of happening.

I didn't ask Fitz about her paternal blank – or I tried not to – I had the vaguest ideas of what it meant to be illegitimate – a romantic bar sinister – I didn't realise she never thought about that – it was her mother, her other pasts, who held the stage of her memory. I could not ask her about them – not yet – instead, I told her about my own vanished father.

'Did he never visit you? Did he never write?' she exclaimed. 'That was lucky.'

'He did visit once. It was awful.'

82

I told her about it – how he had arrived unannounced when we'd been here a few years – maybe the war had already started? – I can't exactly remember. A tall man wearing a dark suit – a businessman – came stooping in under the lintel – twitched off his hat. His face was like an effigy in church – immovably stone – carved from the dead.

'Kezia?' he said – an abrupt clipped voice nothing like what I thought I'd recalled.

'No,' I said. 'Why?'

He said, 'Get your mother' – *authoritatively.*

'She's working.'

'I've come a long way to see you both. Just tell her I'm here.'

'Sorry, I'm not allowed to disturb her in the studio – not for any reason.'

He lost the thin performance of patience which he'd hitherto enacted – threw his hat on the floor – roared in the old thick voice I had remembered – 'Hesketh!'

She was there – her arm across my shoulders – 'It's you' she said. It was not a welcome. They talked for a few sharp sentences – why he was there, what he wanted – ignoring me – I was glad not to be there. I looked at him – a jovial heedless father who I'd sometimes imagined missing – thought *he was always like this*. He only played at being an artist – not like Hesketh. I had only ever seen him in espadrilles but he was used to wearing these patent-leathers for town. He looked at me – I recognised my own high forehead and cheekbones – expecting what?

'Is that all?' he said. 'Can't you even speak to me civilly for five minutes?'

Silence seemed to fill all the spaces between us like something solid.

'No,' I said. 'Just go away.' I only sounded young and rude.

He smiled – I was shocked to see he was missing a tooth at the side, ordinarily – I was about to feel sorry for him when he said, 'You've trained her well, Hesketh. Goodbye.'

I thought she was going to let him have the last word – leave that unpleasant innuendo unchallenged in a dignified refusal to wrangle – but she caught the door open again before he had quite shut it – called after him in her clear bell-toll – 'Bastard!'

I saw the chauffeur's face – scared, amazed, delighted – as he reversed – tried to turn the car quickly as our abuse – loud, fluent, inventive – flew out after the fleeing vehicle – pursuing it like a hawk across the marsh.

Hesketh perhaps guessed that I had hoped for something different once.

'For forgiveness,' she said to me, 'there has to be sorrow first, then understanding, *then* redemption. Not just reappearance.'

'Unless the reappearance itself means those things, like the return of the prodigal?'

'Return of that symbolic sort isn't quite the same as popping back for a visit.'

I laughed – it was liberating laughter, if painful. The next few days were terrible.

It was as well I'd warned Fitz – with the strange synchronicity which haunted my father – (talk of the devil) – a card came from him while she was there – the first since that awful time – I still recognised his handwriting – resented that. It just said that he thought I should write to him as he might soon have to go overseas with his regiment. I showed it to Fitz, who just said, 'Mm, tanks. Rather a sudden impulse after all this time.' Then I showed it to Hesketh. She read it very quickly – moving her head impatiently as her eyes followed the lines in a sort of pantomime of reading – then threw it at me. In the same bell-toll she cried out a litany of insults – not curses, but titles. Fitz looked down and away so as not to witness it.

All afternoon Hesketh drank whisky and cried – there was nothing we could do. When Fitz told her she was well rid of him she agreed, but sobbed out, 'I thought he was part of us but it wasn't real.' It had been like this that first time he came to Saltstreet – only then she was younger – seemed less diminished by it. Late in the evening – when she stood up to get more drink – she folded suddenly to the floor and lay with her head on the muddy doormat – wailing. Between us Fitz and I persuaded – half-carried – her up to bed – covered her with the eiderdown – lay one on either side, holding her.

'I used to love him so much,' she said. 'Oh my dears, don't you leave me too.'

In the cool morning, I woke first. Hesketh was curled up – knees to chin – with her back to me – Fitz's arm was round her shoulders. I was still holding Hesketh's hand – extended backwards to me as though I trotted behind her along a narrow path.

Crambo

The soldiers made such a noise, I couldn't help hearing them, louder than the sounds from inside. I couldn't help watching them, I was enthralled, I crept closer and closer and they never noticed me, even when I was near. They had a radio, and sometimes such music came out of it, everybody danced and the seabirds were frightened away. The tall one, who always crept out holding his head as though he'd just hit it on the way out, the others called Titch, and they laughed at him all the time, I couldn't see why. Whitlow, the one who went running, made me think of a pig, all pink and bristly, but I liked him. He was the one that gave me the beer. The other one was the one in charge, Stevens, he just lay in the dunes with a book whenever it was fine.

After they'd seen me they used to wave at me and try to make me come down, but I wouldn't. They threw biscuits to me, and at night when they had a fire in a brazier they coaxed me to come up close and when I did nothing happened. I thought they might grab me and hit me or spike me or make me eat worms, but they just gave me things. To start with they couldn't realise about my talking and called me Dumby again, until I made them understand Crambo, or something like it. They asked me questions about everything, but I didn't really tell them. I learnt my lesson about telling secrets. They called their hut a nest, or a pillbox, but I thought it was more like a sty or a stable than a nest. Titch said I was their mascot, that was when they gave me the beer and I was sick.

Stevens, my friend, asked me about Kezia all the time, and I told him Hesketh was a witch, and that I was going to marry Kezia before that other one came along. He didn't understand, but it didn't matter. I saw them swimming, Kezia and that other one, and I saw he was a woman. He always wore trousers, either the corduroy ones or the blue ones he'd cut off short now it was hot or the breeches like the land-girls wear, but inside them he wasn't a he, like me. That's why she liked him.

Whitlow teases me sometimes, hard to understand him, but when he wrestled with me I won, he said I was strong, when I lay on top of him and squeezed his throat the others stopped me, they were laughing so much their hands were all feeble. I don't like doing that, it isn't safe, I can't play games like that without winning, accidentally. Titch is kinder, he's exactly like one of the tall wading birds who lift one leg up slowly letting it dangle and stand on their single stilt for a slow time before planting the high leg gradually down. His throat with the bony bump coursing up and down it is like a bird's long neck swallowing water, especially when he sings. He gave me a picture of a girl with a beard, or a man with a girl face and long hair, pointing at their heart sticking out of their chest, with a reproachful expression. I hate it. Whitlow gave me a picture of a girl, definitely, without many clothes on, but I don't like that either, it's the same.

Stevens just sits outside all the time he can, writing in his little book, reading, or marking on papers. He wears glasses then, round ones with thick brown rims, like a nervous thin owl. He tries to talk more than the others. He told me about Dumb Crambo, it's a game, the object of the game is to make people understand the words without saying them, by showing, in mimes, which I can do already very well, but with rhymes. Crambo just means rhyming, making them up, so if the secret word was *cats*, a clue would be *rats bats mats hats slats*. SLATS. I love Crambo. Also Stevens asks me questions, lots of questions, but they always come back to Kezia.

Once I saw him waiting for her on the causeway when she'd gone down to the stile, and he smoked six cigarettes while he was waiting. When he saw her coming he began walking towards her and he took his hat off when he met her. I know what he said to her, he told us all what he was going to say, Good morning, Miss Kezia, would you like some company? I could have told him Kezia wouldn't like that but I didn't, I held my tongue. From where I was in the reeds on the mudflat I could see her shake her head and her mouth make No. No, no, no. And she ran past him along the road, graceful and clumsy and fast as the gypsy foal we once saw running like a rocking-horse on the verge beside the big feather-footed black and white mother horse. He stood looking after her all the way with his mouth open until all her beauty had gone like the last sunlight withdrawn from the evening marsh.

The soldiers' little square-sided circle box made me think of before, before, there was a tower near the beach, past the little creek, where the stream flows out, beyond. It's gone now, nothing left but a ring of flints sticking up out of the earth. That flinty wall all flecked with bricks was round, a circle below as high as Crambo. But above it was all angles, a round made out of flat slats of wood, up up up as high as you can look. The wood was black planks, black like paint but it bites into the wood and makes it dark inside, sticks like that always burn well. I never liked it there, because it had great arms, openwork like a dragonfly's four lattice wings spread wide and pinned up there across across. The wings were all edged with strips of tattered cloth, it looked like a boat's sail when the wind has burst through, ripped it up, snipped it into shreds. Sometimes the gypsies tie little rags like that to a bush so it flutters with cloth fruit, tags of blossom, that's lucky, this wasn't. When the wind was up, the noise of the fabric beating against the wings, tapping at them like a cloud of moths, sounded loud, sounded like something impatient.

I used to see it from far down the beach with its black hood on, its four blasted wings, like a great dark thing standing there. It was close to the beach but back, built on a hard stony tongue like the boathouse. When my ma was a girl there was a lane down that side of the stream, people used to come down with their sacks to the mill tower, it worked somehow, but a flood swept the bank away, it was all empty and deserted, I don't know what they did then. One time one of its arms fell down, trailed on the ground, and she thought we could get some of it for firewood. I was still small then, it was a long way, I didn't like the tower, when we got there I was frightened. We couldn't pull the broken wing down, it was too heavy, still too fixed at the top, it seemed huge up close, but the downstairs door was open just enough for me to squeeze through under the chain, so she made me go in. I didn't want to.

When I was in it was strange inside, round rooms with lots of corners so they could be almost circles, all wood, everything wood like being inside a hollow tree. It smelt of the wood, and of mice and sweet rot. I wanted to get outside again but I knew she wouldn't let me, so I ran up the ladder in the middle, came out in another room the same but smaller, one size down, up again, another size down. At the top, almost, was where the wings joined on, to beams bigger than any tree I've ever seen growing, great vast chunks of wood, solid coffins, straining and juddering like a boat in a gale. Downstairs we hadn't thought of the wind. Up there it was worse than sea force, the whole building was trembling, withstanding it, holding out. I thought it was going to burst apart, fly into nothing, crush Crambo under beams big enough to cover a body, heavy enough to grind it down into sand. I howled but the wind was louder, and the floor drummed under my feet skimpy as a stretched canvas.

I think there was another ladder, shaking flimsy like the twigs that get too thin to climb on when you go up high, then out through a little door onto a narrow platform which ran all round the top. I was a bird. I saw the beach far below, the outland, inland, all beneath. I saw everything different. I looked down on the back of a hawk as it flew by not knowing I saw the hollow of its shoulder blades, I was on a level with the sun. My kingdom, my domain, lay stretched out at my feet. I felt all the joy of being up there, all frightened as I was, up in my tree with the great branches tossing beneath me, groaning and squeaking against each other. I dream about that sometimes, when I'm asleep I'm up there again, watching out. I said to Stevens, your look-out needs to be taller, like a tower, he said I was right.

Then I flew. I climbed across onto one of the wings, it was sticking up just beside me, better than a ladder, all its little flags a-flutter, I stepped out onto it and there was a sort of crunch, grind, something clattered down. The whole thing began to move, it swung me out in a wide arc, round and out, a far flight like a seagull's swoop, like a star shooting through the dark sky in a wild curve on its way to earth a stone's throw below. I landed at my mother's feet, fallen from heaven she said, fallen on my feet like a cat with nine lives. She was pleased because the other limb broke off more when it started to spin round, so we could get at the firewood after all. I wanted to go round again, but she wouldn't let me.

90

Later the whole thing fell down, gradually, bits blew off, bits fell in, it collapsed. We burnt it all eventually until there was nothing left but the flint ring, and the huge bones of beams too heavy for anything but the sea to take away.

When things now are like things then it makes me sad somehow, so I don't like it, it's confusing when I'm asleep, always dreaming of flying.

Meredith

Yes, I did bring you violets, that was no dream. A suitable flower for such an occasion: small, scented, wildish, tenacious of life. (This is my own language of flowers, an unofficial one. To the Victorians I believe violets meant something altogether more forward – if they were fragrant.) You looked – it must be told – you looked disreputable, as though you'd been wounded in a border raid, or perhaps were a highwayman who'd had a brush with the law. This narrow escape, understandably enough, had made you somewhat exalted, as people are who have survived some passage of arms and lived to tell the tale. Perhaps as a result of this intoxication with life you were very gallant; you could be teased a little about that, I think. All your other visitors (do you remember this?) were rather envious of your situation; so dashing to be hurt on duty but at the same time how pleasant to be certain of an extended leave. I felt rather differently, hoping that such injuries wouldn't take too long to heal, knowing they can leave odd scars.

The return of memory is a hopeful sign; they say it waits until we are ready for it, in a kind of wintery hibernation until spring stirs in the mind. Perhaps it is true that this happened more quickly away from the familiar, maybe linked to the body's healing, too? Your recovery is certain now. These mysterious processes continue secretly, as one dreams or sleeps, producing their result as suddenly as card from a conjurer's sleeve. Or so I've found. I walk, as you know, whenever I can; sights strange or familiar seem to be what I seek, but so often afterwards I'm handed the solution to some puzzle, neatly as though I'd picked it up on a scrap of paper in the wind.

For the past is revenant here in London too. On the way to work I pass a piece of waste land, so long covered in fireweed, London Pride and buddleia bushes that it's become an unofficial park. On fine days people sit there to eat their lunch. Yesterday as I went by I paused, intending to lean on a wall in the sun for a moment, and I saw that the whole of the ground was covered in a carpet of flowers, as though it had suddenly remembered what a garden was supposed to be like. It's quite an everyday miracle for the desert to bloom with cornflowers, poppies, wild grasses, speedwell, but it seemed to me then like an omen for the future, that things can remake themselves so unexpectedly.

Everyone misses you, Fitz; will you be restored to us soon?

Crambo

The end of the long shingle spit is the place to look back from, see the whole length of the beach laid out, as the seals see it when they loll on their sandbanks. It takes all morning to walk along, there are three ways you can go, up the middle, the away side or this side. Up the middle is along the spine of the point, where the low dune bumps are laid in a row connected like the bone knobs of a fish skeleton's back. The away side is a steep bank, shale shingle pebble, the sea sweeps past fast to bring more rocks, shovel the ones that are there into neat slopes. Hard walking there, too open with nothing growing, on show to the deep creek entrance and the boats sometimes waiting for the tide so they can ride back up along the channel to the quay. I don't go on that side in case they see me, I stay in the dunes, out of the way. There's nothing along there anyway except stones.

Near side, my side, the dunes shelve shallow down to narrow beaches with grass fringe or smooth pebble edge, sandflats beyond. That's where the birds' nests are, in season, hard to walk along there without treading on eggs, there are so many, all coloured and freckled to look like little oval stones. Those birds don't make a proper nest, they just scrape a hollow for the eggs to lie in invisible. It makes me laugh, you can always tell where the nests are even if you haven't seen them yet, because as soon as you get near the birds will start drawing attention to themselves, trailing a wing pretending it's broken, hopping on one foot, flapping look at me, don't look over there. Crambo knows what that means.

I walk along that side, easy walking, dodge into the dunes if anyone comes along but they don't. Near the end one of the seal banks joins on to the spit when the tide is low, so you can walk up to them as they lie there like giant eggs themselves all dappled with sand. It doesn't upset them, they stay there, after they've looked at me for a minute they take no notice. At the very point, where the water swirls round in a rush when it's coming in, is my look-out place. Outwards, no land, not anywhere. In, there's all the length of beach rolled out small, from the whalebone end to the channel inlet, with the green land billowing up behind.

Before, the beach was empty except for the things that had always been there and the boathouse in the middle as though it had been washed up there. Now when I looked at it, it was different, all covered with wire like matted brambles, as though thorn bushes were spiralling all over it, where they can't really grow. The concrete box was bedded down in the clean sand, swart as a turd, from so far out it looked small enough to shovel away, bury it decently.

Out on the edge the tideline is different, other kinds of things catch on the spit-head, different shells, darker weeds. I used to find all sorts there, out of the sea, once a great tooth as big as my head, a huge branch of pink antlers once. You never know. There are things in the sea not even Crambo dreams about. Everything that came before I could use, nearly everything. Sometimes there was a bit of rubbish, a few things that were dangerous like broken glass, I used to clear it away, put it in a special pit I made where nothing would chance on it. But now there was so much washed up like that, twisted bits of metal, sharp fragments, bunches of rags, gouts of black tar stuck to the stones, unnameable things, far more than the pit would ever hold. It was hard to know what to do, so much to be moved, but where to take it. Even if I put it down into the sinking sand, quake, shiver, swallow it down, it would still be there underneath, hidden but not gone. Sometimes when I was going to sleep instead I thought about what was best to do.

I wish, I wish the sea would come up in a great wave as high as the headland, cover it all up with deep sea bed, start again. I don't dare call it in case it comes, as Hesketh could make it. Even if it swept over us it would be better, we all know that. Only, like the special things the sea brings, pearls and amber nuggets all jumbled in among the smelly filth-packets, there are the Crambos.

I go and wake Stevens up in the night to make him play Crambo and read me rhymes. I stand on the roof and roar and stamp until he comes out holding his eyes in and groaning and he says, 'I was asleep' and I say, '*Deep keep sheep weep*'. I love Crambos more than sweetness. When we play sometimes Stevens cheats, uses words I can't do, like 'silhouette' and I get very angry and shout back at him '*have-a-bet get-a-net you-are-wet*' and he laughs until he leaks out of his eye-corners.

I made up a kind of Crambo to play on my own, like the I spy game Kezia taught me. I look at something, I don't know what it will be, my look just finds it, and I do a Crambo on it. So if it's a shell I go *tell well fell bell knell hell*. HELL!! That's a story, too. Crambos are often stories in between the words if you can find them, but it doesn't matter. They don't have to be.

When I see Kezia threading herself down to the beach, I squat hidden to watch over her until Stevens comes along the dune path, he always turns up. He was going to go down there as well, they all ran up and down my path now without even thinking about it, but I stopped him. I held him round the middle and pulled him back, he called me 'you crazy web-footed half-wit' but I wouldn't let him go and in the end he gave up and we went to look at the tideline. I told him my new Crambos *silt gilt wilt jilt*, he liked them.

It makes me feel happy just that there are Crambos, so many, and new ones all the time. Stevens told me you can get books with lists of them in, nothing but rhymes. After he'd told me that I went and lay on my back with my feet in the air, unfurled, so the sun shone through the triangular pink curtains drawn between the toes, and I rejoiced.

Kezia

In my bedroom were the model cities I'd once made with such dedication – my maps and charts still hung on the walls – all the collections I'd made of fossils or sea-horses – Crambo's gifts of sloughed snakeskins or Roman coins – were displayed on my shelves. Somehow amidst all this Fitz saw the toy theatre – she was prowling round for a book she hadn't read – having asked my permission to look, the theatre distracted her. She exclaimed as though recognising an old friend in a foreign country – delight and disbelief transformed her.

'You've got one of these!'

We lifted it down – Fitz dusted the cardboard proscenium – carefully slid the scenery up and down – set up the footlights – but there was no sign of the actors – put away in a box somewhere, only their wires remained in a neat bundle. She stared at it in silence for a long while – rapt – said, 'I expect you loved playing with this?' I told her about the plays I used to put on for Hesketh – or sometimes with her – the sound-effects – music – elaborate scripts. It brought back some sense of happy occasions – shared pleasure – as though the floodlights were bathing me again in their imagined glow. As for Fitz – I'd never seen her so animated – enthusiasm transformed her. She told me of *her* toy theatre, the attic bedroom where she'd set it up with rows of floor cushions for the audience, the scope of her productions. I could visualise her working alone up there for hours – absorbed – then calling her family upstairs to witness her small magic.

'So you see,' she concluded, 'that was an apprenticeship for my profession.'

I had no idea what she meant until she explained – rather as though I should have known already – that her work was no less than this – theatre in miniature. In all our talks before I'd imagined that her references to plays, props or voices, were on a larger scale.

She said, awkwardly perching on the edge of the table, waving her hands about, 'To me the beauty of the booth theatre is that it's egalitarian, the audience are all in the gods, looking down at the distant illuminated stage from the most magical place in the theatre, yet seeing close detail without their opera glasses, too. The faraway land is near, familiar as childhood's toy proscenium where cardboard melodramas were breathlessly enacted, with the imagination utterly absorbed in an intensity of storytelling. We are lost if reducing the scale does not enlarge the engagement, return us to an innocent state. The romance of gilded barleysugar twists and curlicues, red plush swags, gaslights, will transfer intact to the plain box, the symbolic costume, the makeshift devices; so long as our hearts are in it, the audience will answer *Yes,* be prepared to shout it again louder, when asked if they believe in magic – just for the moment. That's my belief.'

'Oh, yes,' I said. 'Of course.'

It was the first time I'd realised that there were other people – like Hesketh – who had a passion for what they did. It made Fitz seem a different being – to me – but I could hardly imagine her art.

'Could you do a performance for us, here?'

She looked at me – almost madly – for a second – then said 'Why not?'

It was Fitz who asked me what had happened to Crambo – had he gone for a soldier-boy? She was right – he was besotted with the soldiers in a way – fascinated – but I knew he loathed them too – it amused Fitz to think of him teasing them – spying on them – pestering them – as he once had her. But she'd noticed his absence. I answered her that sometimes he vanished inexplicably – for a few days at a time – off on his own devices – or lying up in one of his lairs. Nothing could happen to him here – or, if it did, I would know.

Once – before she came – during the time I could hardly bear to look at him – when he was pretending that Hesketh was a murderer who had threatened him for no reason – I realised something was wrong. It was an indefinable knowledge – like bad weather brewing. I found him early – slumped on the doorstep in the mother-of-pearl pale pre-light – whimpering – holding up one hand as a dog holds up its thorny paw. Hesketh heard him too – never pleased to be dawn woken – she came down with me to open the door – almost grimly. Crambo did not move – did not acknowledge us. I've seen him take sea urchin spines out of his palm with his teeth – suck poison from the sole of his foot – unblinkingly clean cuts in salt water – anneal himself with fire. When he was sick with fever – rarely – he would crawl away to shelter until it had passed – refusing all interference. I could not imagine what help he might seek from us.

Hesketh took his arm – peered at it – hissed between her teeth. My dislike for being near him ebbed away – I came closer to look. The slash on his wrist was so deep – it must have been a glass gash – that inside the red soft gill-opening greyish tubes showed their macaroni ends. He'd made a tourniquet with a twist of rope to stop the bleeding.

'He ought to go to hospital,' Hesketh said.

'He can't.'

We looked at Crambo – who was now holding his wound out with a complacent expression – like a lost dog handed over to the correct authority who must now deal with the problem.

Hesketh sighed.

There was iodine – whisky (for Hesketh) – her neat sampler stitches – sticking plaster over a lint dressing. I overcame my distaste – held his arm still on the table – talked to him while Hesketh persevered with her needle-threading.

'How did you cut it, Crambo? Was it broken glass?'

'Don't know,' he answered dismissively.

He didn't resist – yelped with each pierce – as soon as it was done ran round the yard shaking himself.

'So long as he doesn't want his appendix out,' Hesketh remarked – watching him.

She tried to catch him in time to take the stitches out but he'd bitten them – worried them – off long before. The cut healed well – a red cicatrice gradually flattened into a fine white scar – barely a line. Crambo forgot all about it – remained apparently afraid of Hesketh – banished by me – this ordeal was still his choice though – over other things.

I told Fitz this – I could see she thought of makeshift tabletop surgery as just another of Hesketh's skills – she'd long stopped questioning why about Crambo – she just said that she would keep an eye out for him among the soldiers. I didn't tell her – because I was glad that she wanted to be kind to him – that Crambo was not vulnerable in the ways she might imagine – that the soldiers would do well to keep an eye out for themselves.

Fitz

Broken bones take a long time to heal; broken hearts even longer, I daresay. It would be an exaggeration to call my affliction by that name; I've learnt sorrow before, a hard lesson by rote that I don't intend to rehearse again. (But nothing prepared me for this bitter healing.) Remembering is painful here, too easy while there's nothing else to do. Recently I've lost nothing of greater value than a small, old house, together with the possessions it contained, which once seemed to encapsulate my past. The house still stands, its façade insubstantial as a stage-set, doors and windows opening only into bottomless recollection. My surviving relics – grit-embossed books, glass-scarred furniture – are distributed about the spare rooms of kind friends, or fill gaps in rented flats, awaiting some imagined resurrection. A cardboard suitcase full of dust-caked salvage is all I have left from there. I remind myself that this does not matter.

I have practiced for so long the crucial skill of not thinking, not hoping, not imagining anything good or ill. I have believed, as a matter of faith, that all will somehow be well, but I have not allowed myself to think how it will be. It was better to lose every faculty, to become stupid and dumb, than to feel. But now I remember not only what happened in the raid, but also everything before. I am thawing, so that imagination returns with the other senses. The possibility of restoration seems real, near. I hear news of other people, long lost to each other, who are found again by the liberation of occupied countries, the opening of borders. All there is to be done is to wait.

But the passing of time seems to me very strange in Saltstreet, unlike anything I know; I take it to be another side-effect of exile. Each day lasts so long, measured by such infinitesimal stages, that I glance at the clock three times before it has moved on. Yet, perhaps because the days are so indistinguishable, a week can suddenly have passed, be gone, leaving all exactly as before. (The condition of exile may be like an enforced old age, in which the inevitably slow-paced days speedily make another short-lived year.) Time is essential to heal my injury, a certain number of weeks must pass before improvement can be expected, or even months, but why must that time be so slow to spend? I try to be patient, not only to endure but even to make some use of those essential hours, but it is hard.

With necessary presumption, I think of Ovid banished to the Black Sea, trying to work or write amusing letters, to find enjoyment where he might, but catching himself out, pen poised in mid-air, daydreaming about Rome. I see myself braced in the window seat, book sunk, vacantly staring out at the rain-beaded window, remembering the feeling of home which comes over me in certain streets walking northwards, the ground rising away from the river, toward hills green with trees, glimpsed at all the street-ends. That sense of belonging is my only inheritance. (I look at the clock again, it is still the same.) From this distance I love every brick of my great city, each rattling sash, each shabby balcony. It's as though I stand on the steep hill where I went winter sledging, look out at the long view across the unlikely domes, singing spires and water-towers, dock cranes and gas works, tangled railway lines, the absurd zoo, tall narrow stucco rows of elegantly dilapidated houses, willow-fringed canals, innumerable parks and squares, to the indistinct hills beyond the river valley.

By leaving London when I did, I relinquished something I had never even possessed, but believed in with such devoutness that it seemed true. It comes back to me now: a hope, an expectation, an unspoken wish enclosed in the heart. (Of love, I suppose.) Perhaps that chance need not be lost either, perhaps that moment almost reached can be regained? Even as I chafe for an improvised future that I can't yet imagine, I meditate on all that has passed, try to quench the phosphorus-bomb of rage that smoulders afresh whenever I think of my vanished ones, my broken city, my damaged self. *Nothing is lost,* I mutter, twisting to see the clock again.

It is high summer at last. I have received an invitation to go to a concert party for convalescent officers, at a great house along the coast; I may bring a guest. I asked Hesketh if she'd like to see the famous gardens, eat strawberries on the lawn. She wanted Kezia to go instead: 'It's time she went to a party'.

'But,' she added, 'whatever will you wear?'

I said that was perfectly fine; I'd wear what I always wore. Kezia was the problem. She could hardly go in her ragamuffin beach clothes. Hesketh took us into her bedroom-alcove off the studio where a wardrobe built into the angle of the attic roof is stuffed far beyond its capacity with satin evening pyjamas, Chanel check wool suits, Riviera cocktail gowns, Venetian silk wraps; relics of a different life, all quite unsuitable for Kezia.

'Shall we look in the loft?' Kezia asked hopefully.

In the corner of the studio ceiling, a trapdoor opened into this loft, more of an elongated roof-cupboard, another of Saltstreet's secrets. I stood on a chair, passed boxes down, until Hesketh said, 'Try that one.' It was a monogrammed canvas demi-trunk, all Colonial bamboo, exceptionally heavy. Inside was an atrophied Harris Tweed coat which Hesketh thought might be useful when we had persuaded it to unbend. Beneath were various embalmed boating-shoes, a rolled panama which started to crumble when I put it on my head, a pile of linen summer clothes.

'Whose are these things?' I asked, perhaps unwisely.

'It's just Giles's holiday clothes,' Hesketh said, airily. 'Don't worry; he told me many times to use anything here – I very much doubt he recalls their existence, anyway. He was a bit of a dandy at Deauville in the 'twenties, but I fear he wouldn't fit into them now.'

With a flourish she shook out a Madras seersucker bathing robe in checks of turquoise, indigo, mustard, violet, smelling strongly of stale lavender-bags.

'We could make a summer frock for you out of this, Kezia.'

Kezia appeared startled at this colourful vision of herself, but it was a clever idea – after a washday, much stitching and constructing, she is transformed. It's bright, not childish yet not over-sophisticated; nothing princessy about it, as I pointed out. I have a blazer, some once-impeccable linen trousers which I just cut off to length, one of those striped Breton jumpers which were so fashionable once but not yet incomprehensible; a vast haul, myriads of coupons' worth. Hesketh understands the importance of dress; she was casual about her bounty ('you may as well have these'), but I feel complimented that she considers me a candidate for such sartorial flourishes. I have never really learned to travel light: people are always too generous.

The offcuts of bright fabric add to my store of raw materials, the things I've begun to collect since Kezia asked me about the little theatre. I'm handicapped in making my imagination manifest by lack of tools, basic supplies, not technical skills. A limited palette (or a censored stage) may stimulate invention, but a mere shortage of nails can be frustrating, even in a rough and ready theatre. But I improvise, make do. It does not matter; I am enjoying myself. There is an intoxicating sense of powers returning. Crambo doesn't bother to spy on me any more; as I hammer away in the yard I almost miss him.

As I wandered about looking for jetsam which might inspire me, an idea came to me as the real ones do, slowly, forming ineluctably with the gradual illumination of dawn, where the first greening light inevitably increases to the full intensity of sunrise. Not all at once but gently it rose, taking its due time, but it was there among the dunes that I first sensed that early glimpse of future day, a stumbling wondering about making a Saltstreet *Tempest*. I wrote to Meredith, the poet, trusting that invisible ink idea to paper where it might become legible to the right reader. I told her that I was trying to make another miniature theatre, although it would be rough, from some of Hesketh's wine-boxes, smooth light wood with sliding lids, easily cut. There is plenty of planking wood on the beach for a solid frame if I need it, paint from Hesketh, cloth-scraps from Kezia, the random riches of the whole tideline for a props cupboard. This was the technical side; I made it sound easy. I asked her what she thought about Shakespeare combined with Punch and Judy, Pollock's toy theatre, these our inanimate actors. She answered with questions, suggestions, seriousness. The process has begun.

Meredith

About your work, a new Tempest. *Oh, my dear. Perhaps we should have guessed that a spell of exile would bring about strange new enchantments from you, the dreams of the dispossessed. In theory 'all Boets and Bainters' should be sent off to other worlds in order that, when they return, they can bring back with them tales of far-off places – the dark continents they've visited, those they have explored in their own selves. In practice it doesn't always work, but I have a feeling that you must be one of those who comes back to the city like a Marco Polo, ships' holds crowded with enough cargo to keep you in adventurous merchandise for the rest of your life. Incidentally, how much more comforting it must be to have Shakespeare as your castaway companion rather than the Bible, which would be far less to the purpose: all that magnificent language about absolute nonsense – abominations, begats, forbidding magic cushions under one's armpits. Whereas with your complete W. S. to hand your every imagined destination is described, mapped, illuminated, however far in the interior.*

I remember so well watching your show on the boat, so drawn into the microcosm of that complete yet miniature world that your voice – so recognisable – seemed to issue from these odd actors who were so fragile yet so gallant, as are people. Your hands were sometimes visible above, manipulating the figures with extraordinary dexterity of course – but also tenderness. Your skill was so out of the ordinary that it lifted the performance into a realm of feeling which was nothing but miraculous. Their faces appeared to move, to alter with emotion, their gestures, walks, mannerisms were so well-observed, so truly communicated, that it was impossible not to believe that you had animated them, breathed some of your soul into those mandrake actors, so that for the duration they shared your life. (But they're not like ventriloquists' dummies, crammed with malice, only awaiting their chance to speak evil: they remind me more of the Greek shadow-puppets with their air of immense if mischievous good nature, who are yet undoubtedly inanimate outwith their performance.)

All of them have a sadness, contain the poignance that for all their shared characteristics they are not human, however skilfully they enact a simulacrum of that condition. And all of them seem sad for us, since that humanity which they can't share is the quality which makes us mortal. Denied life, they are also without death. Your actors are exquisitely made, clearly: expressive, arrestingly strange – but by what mystery do you make them so heartfelt? We the audience have no defences, we accept these creations of balsawood or paper at their own valuation, as creatures of spirit. All the fugitive qualities we search for at the play, half-hope to find – atmosphere, subtlety, integrity – are simply there. At what deep well of childhood make-believe you bring us all to drink, so after the draught we perceive everything with the absolute vision of that lost world. I believe you could produce anything, any great play, any epic poem, with such a troupe to bring it to the stage.

Mad Prospero, yes. Don't you think, in our lives as they are now, redemption has to be different, less cut-and-dried, perhaps? Can Prospero not negotiate a new contract with his chick, so that Ariel stays with him but is free – and Prospero will have to love him differently? Then they can stay on the island. (Before, Prospero only had to give up the island too because of that tiresome Miranda, aside from justice being done, lessons learnt, the pattern re-established, and all made *well. This may be over-optimistic nowadays – too much reconstruction? She might marry Caliban (who could double with Ferdinand); there's redemption and transformation scene in one. The beast turns into a prince when she kisses him – but of course he's a prince already, isn't he? Though of a different land. Your Ferdinand could be another cross-dressed king's daughter, but he's the hero, he can't retire to the island, he must come home.)*

This is unravelling the plot, I realise, perhaps unacceptably – but it is interesting to make the sacrifice not a simple relinquishing, but a purposed change of character – so much more difficult to maintain. (One thinks of the ease of giving up sugar, say, during Lent, compared with the positive resolve to be charitable – far worse.) This raises new problems of casting – yes, I see what you mean about type, but it isn't always simple. Your problems and solutions must be quite different from the usual run, from what you say. Apparently we require at least one limping Caliban, one handsome prince (or similar), one ethereal spirit, one islanded princess, one ruined mage, so on. But with your production, can the roles be more fluid? Prospero should certainly be female, like God…

I agree it's profoundly true that Prospero can't combine being a magician with having his dukedom back, not both spiritual and temporal power, but now he'd never settle to court life. But do you think he's relieved to give up his art, not struggle any more? Or do you think he's miserable in Milan, always trying out conjuring tricks at dinner and mooning about missing Ariel? Has he achieved enlightenment by abjuring his rough magic? Or was the enchantment just an interim measure, so they could return from the island, to their reality? There are no answers to these questions, or if there are they don't matter. It's all illusion; the play's the thing.

III

Fitz

I write my hopes, my plans, my theories, in letters now; my words not so much like a message in a bottle. I think it amused Meredith too, my account of cutting off some of Giles's trousers to make more shorts, then regretting it. The ragged edges looked eccentric, I was aware: when I met Corporal Stevens on the beach he seemed rather startled. But he rallied quickly, asked me for a light – which I could hardly refuse, but gave him hoping that Kezia wouldn't see us, accuse me of consorting with the enemy. He spoke to me eagerly, ignoring all the ridiculous aspects of our situation, saluting me as his superior officer in spite of my garb, deferring to me about my 'wound'. When he asked me to tell Kezia about him, adding wistfully, 'She seems keen on you,' I answered that in recompense he appears to be Crambo's particular favourite.

Curiously, it did not take a moment to realise that Kezia would in theory have something in common with this perfectly nice youth. He seems isolated, separated from his companions by his bookishness, well-spokenness, mild background (his father is a vicar). His taste in reading is as old-fashioned as hers; he writes poetry of a traditional kind. These confidences came tumbling out. What I could not explain to him is that Kezia will never take any notice of him because of what he now is. No point in telling *her* that such soldiers are choiceless fellow-victims; she will never acknowledge them, for to do so would be to collude with their warped view of her inviolate world. Stevens is, as Hesketh remarked to me, destined to remain a minor character.

I try to conjure our other familiar or resident elemental for Meredith; with the coming of full summer, Crambo's boating season has begun. He has a variety of vessels, all unmistakably Crambo craft ('Cramboats', as Kezia calls them), each suitable for a different mood, perhaps – of his or the sea's. The first time I saw him on the water he was astride an old oil barrel, riding it like a triton on a dolphin, with his feet resting on side-panels or running boards as though they were stirrups. He paddles this primitive device with an ordinary paddle, rather disappointingly: a broken oar he no doubt found washed up on the beach, and which he plies arbitrarily to either side with a kind of demented skill. As well as bobbing about on this marine see-saw, he has a contraption both more elaborate yet more eccentric: a catamaran-style pair of long basketwork cocoons down which he can extend his legs to skim across the water surface with insect-like darting motions. Fortunately, neither staying dry nor afloat seem to be major preoccupations; he accepts both gradual submersion and sudden capsizement with equanimity, shaking himself like a dog when he regains dry land, or remounting his craft if he can right it. (There is more grit to Crambo than I first realised.)

The strangest sight of all, perhaps, is Crambo's gondola – again, Kezia's name for it: a raft that he stands up in to row with an odd figure-of-eight stroke he has invented, using a crooked post. Because the platform is very low in the water like an overloaded punt, he can only use it on the calmest days, when he crosses our horizon apparently borne footsure on the water, making elaborate gestures with his hands before him, like a conjurer's preliminary passes. To see him sometimes sink with such composure, sometimes guffaw at his good progress, is to agree with Kezia's observation: he deserves to walk on water, if anybody does.

The great occasion of Kezia's birthday coincided with what they call 'good news' about the war. She is, to my amazement, twenty-one; her coming-of-age was a poignant occasion, as it turned out. To celebrate, Hesketh herself made a remarkable pie, which she called Stargazey (though it was only faintly related to the pies that are so called in Cornwall). It was a wrecker's dish, filled with a mixture of fish, flesh and fowl; there was cheese within, entire eggs in their shells, vegetable layers, different sauces, while herring heads peered upwards through the pastry in a disconcerting shoal. (I see where Kezia's cookery comes from.) At dinner Hesketh wore a sweeping crimson ballgown, had her hair up. Kezia sans Rapunzel looked like a cabin boy in her new frock, especially when she recited an impromptu ode. Even I dressed up for the occasion, in one of Giles's tattered jazz-age silk shirts. Hesketh somehow found a bottle of champagne, slightly ambered with age, for us to drink Kezia's health. I had put some thought into finding her a suitable present, had a parcel of books sent from London; she was polite but I can tell she would have preferred – I don't know what – something else. She seemed a little disappointed. Hesketh gave her many things: scent and a watch and books and a locket and a portrait of herself – Hesketh in a frame.

(This self-portrait I looked at again today, by daylight – an extraordinary painting. There's something medieval about the wood panel it's on, slightly curved with the warp of the tree, the timber grain visible through the thick vivid paint, but the formal hierophant pose is that of an unknown Elizabethan. Hesketh looks steadily out – one almost thinks 'unblinking' – regal, idol-like, her wild hair caught back severely, her blue paint-spattered overall elaborate as a richly patterned embroidered gown. In her hands she holds, like emblems of power, the orb of her jewelled palette, the sceptre of a thick brush. Behind her, through the window, is the sea; a miniature of her realm glimpsed in the background. At her feet, heraldic yet alive, reclines a black dog. The strength of her gaze blasts out of the picture in a gale force high enough to blow the viewer back. Beautiful, strange, the image tires the eyes to look at it too long, and draws them back again.)

After dinner there were rather dated dance records on the wind-up player, an uproarious card game which revolved around smuggling contraband through customs, other traditional festivities. My hosts vibrated in their own closed world, fine as the anchor-lines and rigging trembling on a ship in a glass bottle, while I watched anxiously the thing so distant, precious, fragile, which they shared with me so freely, all unawares. Hesketh must have been drinking in the studio as well as while she cooked; I had to help her up the stairs. When I came back down Kezia said to me, defiantly, 'She's only tired.'

'Of course,' I said. 'Of course.'

As I stood outside for my final cigarette, I prayed that nothing will harm these two who seem so vulnerable; I vowed that I will not, at least. Enough sadness must inevitably come.

I also promised myself that once back at home I will take some friends, or perhaps just one friend, just Meredith, to Soho, to Bertorelli's restaurant, one evening after the theatres have gone in, at dusk, when the soft rain glitters on the window glass like pantomime stardust, the puddles reflect street-lamps glowing as footlights. We'll have one of the corner tables in a dim booth, under the framed photos scrawled with autographs, with a banquette familiarly upholstered in the angular patterned scratchy plush of a tube bench, out of the way of the crowd. There will be cheap heavy wine in a straw-covered bottle, plates of spaghetti generously studded with garlic, scattered with cheese, followed by excellent coffee. This meal, with variations on the theme, has haunted me before, but never with such hallucinatory power. It appeared to me so vividly that I could smell that particular desirable mixture of garlic, alcohol, coffee, cigars, Londoners' damp coats, life.

That yearning, commonplace enough now, when such simple delights have long been so hard to obtain for so many, was the first time I've associated my homesickness, my urgent wish to return, with a deeper anxiety: the dreadful thought that life might go on without me, a red double-decker bus speeding away down Piccadilly, its familiar promise receding until the would-be traveller is forced to admit that it's gone, we've missed it.

Sometimes at night here in Saltstreet when my lamp is safely out I open the window, look out, to torment myself, I suppose. I like to think that the same stars, when I can see them, shine down on us all. Some nights, when the moon is up bright, the cloud not curtaining the sky with an officious blackout, the marsh and all the inlets of the creek, the distant church tower, the inland hill, are illuminated with that strange white floodlight, an otherworldly silver mirror to daytime. Colour is muted, but shadows crisply thrown, all the detail of water ripple and reed bed clear, picked out exactly by the dousing moonlight. Those nights I find most difficult. I've always been a vehement character, one to act on my feelings, go to knock on the door with a petition for the beloved, not stand on the step all night long. I'm a flower-bringer, letter-writer; love possesses me as a permanent occupation to be pursued, red-bloodedly. Yet there seems to be nothing I can do with my nascent passion but bottle it up for future use.

It was past midnight when I looked out and saw, instead of the usual unlit landscape, fires on the marsh. These weren't the blue flickers of will-o'-the-wisp marsh gas, but ordinary human flames in the darkened country, camp-fires, oil lanterns. They looked both too efficient and discreet to be Crambo devices, yet similarly lawless. It was a strange sight after all the years of banished light; briefly I wondered if they could be bonfires of celebration, victory beacons, but the land was silent. The thought of rousing Hesketh from her high-pillowed sleep seemed impious – it was obscurely impossible to consider wakening Kezia. So I did nothing, but watched the little red-gold flickering light as though it came from somewhere else, from the first people on earth who knew the secret of fire, or the legionaries who are said to haunt the hill, or whoever else was lost in that dim place between the two elements.

This morning, I'd forgotten, although I still had the sense that there had been some dream to make the morning unreal. Then Kezia told me, so matter-of-fact, that the gypsies have come. They appear every year, she says, with their piebald circus ponies, dodgy-smelling stews, mercenary compliments, lucky clothes-pegs. People come from miles about to have their fortunes told, their knives sharpened, their saucepans welded, their purses lightened. I have decided to walk over there, visit the gathering, see if I can buy a bunch of white heather for Meredith – but in the evening, when the caravans are lighted, the sense of fairground foreignness at its height. And someone may tell me that I have a lucky face.

Crambo

I realised that Stevens had tricked me. Kezia wouldn't go off with that other one, that woman, she'd never marry *him*. But maybe Stevens she might, now he was my friend. *Friend lend.* I'd seen him making up to the trouser woman too. *Mend tend.* So he was trying to get into the boathouse, betray me, his friend, and marry Kezia without me, on his own. I told him she was a selkie, that if she married anyone she'd leave them and go back to the sea, be a seal again, abandon them forever to cry all alone. But he didn't understand me, or believe me. *Rend send end.* I decided to kill him, put him out of the way. She wouldn't care, she'd be glad. I didn't have Hesketh's gun, or the black dog, but it didn't matter, I could do it anyway.

I had to wait days and days before he was in the right place. He came down to the sea as usual, the sea was far in so he took his kit off in the dunes and ran down the path through the soft high sand, which was my path anyway, and when I saw him bare except for those baggy swimming trunks I hated him and was sorry for him at the same time, but it didn't stop me. My aim is true. I threw the rock exactly onto one of the flat upside-down plate shapes which the sand makes on top of the mines, just beside him, and hit it with a noise I could feel, hammer on stone. He screamed, high as a bat, and the whole of the air in front of me rose up into a wall of beach.

I ran away back into the dune-pockets and lay on my back kicking all my legs to laugh better, laugh too much to breathe. Clumsy Stevens, not looking where he was going, silly Stevens.

I saw them all three of them even Her, Hesketh, who never goes out now, not beyond the yard, walk off down the causeway, off on an outing. The trouser one was in the middle, she had one of them on each arm, one of those old ketch barges with the tall sail and the small sail billowing each way. *Sail tail quail mail fail wail.* I knew they were off to visit the gypsies, I'd been already, eaten my stew, given them the things I keep for them when I find them, taken the special tea for my ma which they always bring her. They smell of gunpowder like me, like the marsh does now, acrid, savoury, burnt, not like anything else, lovely lovely.

The gypsies are all related, one tribe, all called something Burton, but they don't notice like the seals all being seals together without noticing. The oldest lady tiny under her cartwheel hat reminds me of a mushroom, small stalk underneath the wide shade. She doesn't mind me, she liked my Crambos. Some of the others don't like the people who aren't gypsies to be different, they want all the others to be all the same as each other, so they can tell who's who. Kezia used to sing me a song *I'm off with the raggle-taggle gypsies-o* but they wouldn't like many people to go off with them, not me, not Trousers, maybe not even Kezia. All the separate people have to stay separate, it doesn't work if they join together. Phoebe Burton is the Mother, she likes Hesketh, she's like Hesketh. Hesketh painted her picture once, I saw it because She did it outside, it was big, the wild sky came halfway down like it does behind the hill with the white road running down it, all the trees shuffled together at the bottom, in front the caravan decorated all over with the bright colours faded and dusty, half the horse looking the other way and Mrs Phoebe sitting on her steps wearing a red shawl, smoking her long pipe. There was everything in that picture, the exciting smell and all the places they've been to, returned to, the road going on and on, the caravan creaking and swaying, the lines in her

117

face like the deep roads they all travel. A magician's picture, it was dangerous, a spell of longing, it made me want to go with them, even though Crambo could never go away, not from the island. It made Mrs Phoebe laugh, she said it made her look like a duchess.

They all came running out to greet Hesketh, all of them, the old lady, Duchess Phoebe, her three daughters in their red bloomers, her dark shifty sons-in-law, the bakers' dozen of wren-brown children. When they all smiled you could see their golden teeth, their pockets were full of coins as well as knives to jingle, they all drank from the bottle Hesketh had brought, out of tin mugs all painted like boats. Later they sang, some of them danced, one of the girls put a red flower into Trousers's buttonhole and everyone laughed. The black dog wasn't anywhere. They stayed for hours after it got dark, no one came when they lit their lamps. No soldiers came out any more *boom doom tomb* but anyway the gypsies are invisible, too untidy to see.

I waited until they came back along the causeway, to see them home safely. Hesketh hadn't brought Her gun. Kezia was smiling, talking, Trousers kept hold of them both even when they all went dancing a few steps, they were so happy to have been gypsies for one evening. I think the Burtons were pleased to see them as well, with their drink and their presents, but you can't tell.

Kezia

I was looking out from the top step of our rough stairway down to the sea – the place which I used to call my lookout – where I made weather observations for my log when I was a child. It was one of those days when the waves are close in – the sea is cross-hatched – finely chopped blue-grey cabbage texture – it moves so fast – brightly – evenly – it's like a clockwork machine – a child's wind-up toy of tumbling waves in perpetual motion. The light catches each point of water – evenly spaced – a neat pattern of flashing triangles disposed across the entire ocean – a pretty sight yet – as Fitz said – implacable. When the sea is like that I always think the dark shades in the wave-troughs are seals' heads – 'the principle of camouflage' – Fitz again. Benbow dismisses such illusions – though it is hard to find a single place with a telescope – without any distinguishing mark to move from. That morning, I thought a dark fin broke the water.

Far out – those big fish stay in the deep water – it was another dark triangle – a low-flying pennant – perhaps an illusion. But through the glass it was unmistakable – it moved at a different pace from the phantom fins. Hesketh – I looked up at the studio windows – she smiled down at me – pointed. It had not been a good day for her so far. I went indoors – found Fitz slowly putting away the breakfast – made her come out. I half-expected the thing to be gone – for a moment I thought it had vanished – then she saw it.

'There!'

Distant – impossibly close – its fierce tacking in the wild blue waters was like a storm – with that thrill of fear which yet acknowledges pleasure. Fitz stared at it through Benbow for a long time – her face puckered up with the squint –

serious as a look-out for submarines. Politely she handed it back to me – stared out again with her hand shading her eyes. It's a strange trick that instrument plays – not only enlarging the subject but clarifying it – so that the colours jump into jewel focus – enamel-bright – the disc-shaped picture vividly unreal – a lunette in a picture book. I never quite believe what I see through it – I thought Fitz felt the same.

'When something stirs in the deep,' she said, 'maybe it's life. Still out there after all.'

'Like a flag waving to us?'

'Yes, exactly. A signal flag.'

Perhaps I looked doubtful – for in a moment she added – 'Our distant selves appearing to us like wild travellers?'

I nodded – we both looked back at the dark sign in the flashing water – but it had gone – there was only the constant pattern of the sea – still making the natural camouflage which Fitz told me was just a vagabond word – a slang smokescreen – lawless bandits' cant for the whiff of disguise.

When Fitz's performance was ready she gave it to us as a special evening – an entertainment, not exactly her usual work. Hesketh told me it was important we should understand this – rather as though she had to give an exhibition in a strange place with only makeshift materials for her use. It must have been close to the longest day – no – later in the summer – but still those long blue evenings twilit until midnight – when the white stones and the foam shine light in the dusk. We ate outside – a celebration dinner – eel consommé followed by a clam risotto and summer pudding – the eels swam in their jellied undersea clarity – the clam shells lay on their pale shingle mounds – a sea feast.

Fitz's booth was set up in the yard like a Punch and Judy

show – the little box of the stage glowed with footlights she'd made from glass eggcups full of lamp oil – the proscenium arch was fantastically decorated with gilded cockle shells. Her audience included most of the Burton tribe – connoisseurs of outdoor entertainment – disposed on various makeshift benches – with Crambo lurking at the back like the traditional ticketless fugitive from justice. Hesketh and I perched on kitchen stools, gripping each others' hands tightly, as the stage floated before us like a magic window. Fitz's familiar hoarse, drawling voice announced the play – her hands entered the enclosed space – the curtain rose. The scene was a harbour town – the driftwood template of quayside houses made us all gasp – the uneven wood made the line of their roofs – the windows were illuminated – the pub sign swung – there were shop names inscribed with Victorian flourishes – posters for the event we were watching – *The Sailor's Return* – all with a period touch which prepared us for outrageous melodrama.

The first actor swept on – a starfish-faced sailor, button-eyed, rope-haired, tattooed arms akimbo, his sky-blue cardboard hat lettered MARINER – he spoke with bravado in swashbuckling verse – much of which, to Crambo's audible satisfaction, rhymed. As our hero stood on the dock freshly disembarked, the lighthouse in the distance began to blink – the high sea appeared over the harbour wall. A spirited storm ensued – billowing corkscrewed blue teatowels – wild applause – from the waves a mermaid rose, seated on a shell like Venus. Her tail was a sweep of scaly silver lamé – her body a whittled blue bowling skittle – her hair the finest seaweed – her mirror a silver coin bearing the minute legend MARINA. She was a creature of eccentric charm with whom the sailor was understandably infatuated at first sight. There could be little doubt that they were made for each other, although she uttered some doubts at first about the legendary infidelity of mariners – he about mermaids' unpleasant habit of luring sailors to their doom. As their first declarations were made their idyll was interrupted by a convincingly ghastly sea monster which rose suddenly from the deep behind them. It was some time before they became aware of this threatening presence constructed from components of crab claws, overlapping oyster shells jointed together, stacked sea urchin cases – a spiny sea-dragon – every time they looked round it sunk out of sight. This suspense was (I think) judiciously ended early when Crambo's audible agitation became too extreme – whether he was anxious on the sea monster's behalf or about the results of its behaviour – who can say? The creature attempted to come ashore – the sailor repulsed it – the mermaid enchanted it – eventually it was brought to order by a chorus of *Rule Britannia* in which we all joined with gusto. The monster was reformed – remembered it was British – sunk down – the mermaid and the sailor swore eternal love and perpetual happiness.

I cried with delight and amusement – Hesketh shouted 'Brava!' – the Burtons applauded until the marsh echoed. In the traditional manner, Fitz's face appeared startlingly – filling the stage – as she acknowledged her tribute. Clapping – cheering – still laughing – how else could we tell her of the burden of tenderness we felt for her creations, so vulnerable yet robust, speaking such supple words from their still faces, somehow more poignant than living performers.

'It was sheer genius,' Hesketh whispered to me. 'The gods descended unexpectedly.' Then, as Fitz appeared perspiring from her backstage cupboard, 'Why didn't you tell us you could do this, Fitz? You are a true artist, my dear, if a very unusual one.'

122

Fitz smiled – sketched a bow – shyly for her – said, 'I was going to do *The Tempest*, but it's not ready yet, not for here. And perhaps *A little saint best fits a little shrine ...*'

'This is perfect for here and now. It is all inspired – the actors, too.'

What we did not say – it was all of a piece – the rollicking words went with the leading pair – funny, even bizarre, yet utterly irresistible – I had never seen anything like it.

'You must keep them,' Fitz said to me. 'They belong here by the sea, I think, in their happy-ever-after.'

She shook hands with her entire audience – except poor distant Crambo – with the air of an old stager – openly pleased, yet oddly modest – not so much barnstorming swagger as simple pleasure.

It was that night as I lay under only a sheet – heard Fitz moving quietly about in her room – that I thought I could not bear for her ever to go away – leave me behind with only those two weird figures for company.

Meredith

My dear, I saw a painting of Hesketh's, quite by chance, in a gallery (of sorts) by the BM; it was sensational. The colours were unique, in the true sense of unlike any others, all freshly invented; the brushwork was Amy Johnson when she's flying, the wooden panel looked like something Byzantine. It was the most extraordinary subject: two children crouching inside a hollow tree stump, hunched over a treasure trove of coins in a jar, completely absorbed in their find. They are like twins, only opposites rather than identicals, but both strange beyond description, otherworldly yet of the earth earthly, elementals in human form perhaps. Their extreme youth, outwardly and physically at least, contrasted with the ancientry of their hoard, its history of measurable age within human lifespans, to make the most striking image. I've thought of nothing else all day. The dealer titled it 'Memory', but that may not be its original name. It was sold. Now I might say the colours all looked as though they had just been dug out of the earth too: ochre, umber, sand, ordure, sea-clay, bark, lichen… I coveted that painting.

They had another – earlier, they said – which was quite different: bold, fairground colours, a glorious Mediterranean view, not at all faux-naïf but full of joy, the Northern joy in that sunscape. It would have made a perfect stage set for a Shakespearean comedy, a pastoral idyll set in an island kingdom we all know but will never visit except in the imagination, but then we'll go there often. (The coast of Bohemia, perhaps?) It would be more comfortable to live with than the other one, less haunting.

Seeing these makes me understand what you've told me about Hesketh far more. Of course she recognised you as kindred, another of those who are blessed or doomed to do their best without expecting the slightest understanding, let alone reward (of the commercial kind, at least). I add that hastily because I know that you would rather give your Tempest on a beach, in a disused room, under a bridge arch, to an audience of a few who were moved by the magic, than be paid fortunes to perform to the indifferent. Luckily, I feel the same; we are also able, with our dark art, to give play and poetry to the starving hearts who never knew they needed it till now. (Of course, we may go hungry in the process, but that is the artist's task. We are nourished by what we do anyway, as surely as workers in a pie-and-mash shop, so can't complain.) O Fitz, when I saw those paintings by Hesketh I felt such fellow-feeling! Very humbly, for she has realised her vision, I recognised a mutual starting point on that long journey which is the one we've chosen. Does it go too near the heart of the mystery to say this?

Kezia

All the officers in the locality were invited – as well as all the convalescents already staying in the hospital wing of the great house – the concert was to be broadcast. Hesketh was absolutely determined that I should go – as though she had suddenly noticed that I had done nothing like that since I was eleven years old – as though it mattered. She told me that people always went to garden parties in July. It seemed extraordinary to me to think that there could be something going on fifteen or twenty miles along the coast – or further – and we would just go. It stunned me rather that we might get there from Saltstreet – on a bus. I hadn't left the place more than a few times in ten years – even Hesketh's absences had grown fewer – shorter – though no less inexplicable. Now it seemed such things were possible. In my new clothes I felt less like a bony child – more effectively disguised.

On the journey, Fitz was sweet to me – solicitous but not fussy. She could walk without her stick now, though she still carried it – seemed somehow taller – was tanned, which suited her. The infrequent bus along the coast road was not full yet – the journey felt exciting but not frightening – the sea stayed in sight. Fitz talked about going to London together one day – all of us – taking the train – theatres, restaurants, parks. I thought Hesketh would love it. We ate our sandwiches less than halfway there, peering out through smeary glass windows at dusty country. The house – our destination – was familiar from many pictures when we came to it – run aground on a hillock in a bland park. The bus paused incongruously at the enormous gates – open today – a long way off down an avenue of chestnuts the house was there again. We were ferried along the drive in a cart – some people were taken in cars but we

126

preferred to ride with the flat-backed horse.

There were people everywhere – Fitz saw how much I was taken aback by the numbers – she said she hadn't realised it would be so busy. Fitz looked at these people as though they were a flock of birds (I thought) – a gathering of curlews – comprehendible as a mass of similarity. To me – as yet – this was impossible – each one was a fellow creature like myself – or Hesketh – who should be separately hailed – greeted – acknowledged. Many of them were in uniform of some sort – they seemed almost oddly jolly – although some were on crutches or visibly injured in some way all were, as Fitz put it, 'on the mend'. She agreed with me that it was strange for there to be so many people in the same place that it was impossible to know them all – but she told me to think of them like the swans – who sometimes flock in such numbers – a great company could fly over without pausing – or some might land in a field – nest on the marsh – become our neighbours – so we might make friends with them – but could never expect to know all the swans who had passed. This thought helped me to remain quietly there – pretending to myself that I was in a field of wild birds who would not notice me or mind my presence.

At the doorway a woman glanced at the invitation very casually – directed us to go in and find ourselves a place. It was all happening in a long room filled with an assortment of chairs set in haphazard lines facing one end. We chose two modest Windsor chairs in a row of them which might have been borrowed from the kitchen – set near the windows – settled down to examine the room. I remember every detail – parquet floor – long windows open but with shades down against the bright sun – the small wooden acorns on their cords drawn inexorably back and forth across the floor with the blinds' slow breathing – a frieze high round the walls painted the same blue as Hesketh's Wedgwood box. At the stage end the room curved – there were gilded books put away behind grilles – a monumental grand piano – a balustraded gallery above encircling more shelves. Dramatic young men in their shirtsleeves were arranging microphones – unreeling cables – directed by equally stagey women with clipboards. This (I thought) Fitz actually *likes*. This is her world. She could easily be up there with them – her shirt collar unbuttoned like that – her sleeves rolled up – if one of the mikes needed adjusting she'd stick her cigarette in her mouth – narrow her eyes – enthusiastically spin the wheel on the side of the stand – test the height by saying some quote down it – imitating an actor whose mannerisms I wouldn't recognise – so that all the others would laugh.

When the room was full – after some delay – the music began. A quite elderly, very smart woman played the piano – Debussy, Chopin, Beethoven – she played well. I remembered going to concerts in Paris as a child. Time seemed to curve round from this sunny sad afternoon to the dark vivid concert hall – all the life I'd lived in between shrank – telescoped into miniature. There did not seem to be any reason why that moment – with its music – should come to an end. But there was silence – stirring – applause – and it was over.

During the interval – still floating in that strange time-free state – I followed Fitz back out onto the lawns – she went to fetch us cups of tea. I watched her in the queue outside the marquee – lounging with her hands in her trouser pockets – sleeves rolled up – now smoking. I saw a woman – a proper woman – silk-shirted, black linen-suited, with a long knotted rope of pearls – see Fitz from a distance – become somehow different – walk up to her. Fitz looked surprised – blushed

– was changed. I noted the way they stood together – Fitz braced – her friend fluid – not touching each other – yet connected. It wasn't possible for me to understand why I felt such desolation – or even to be sure if that was what I felt – or whether it was merely pain at the wreckage – so much mortality in the bright sunshine.

That morning following, the cloth-of-gold brocading of the marsh-inlets was overlaid by a lake of tin tray-smooth water only broken by the tallest reed heads. Swans swam unconcerned across our invisible drowned causeway – an unforgettable inundation. I imagined the machine gunners stranded uselessly on the dunes – their castle underwater. Hesketh was delighted – expansively jolly even at breakfast – when I pointed out that Fitz hadn't been able to get back – was lost somewhere – she dismissively assured me that she'd be perfectly fine. Hesketh was far more deeply struck by how good it had been of Fitz to bring me home – went on unnecessarily (I thought) about this accompanying as such a great kindness. Was Fitz escort or chaperone I asked – acidly – on duty either way.

Rather like the morning after the ball in books I'd read but not really understood, Hesketh asked me questions with apparent quicksands of meaning quaking under smooth paths. On matters of light – colour – shades – hues – I was well-trained to answer – I knew also the architecture of the house – the dates of the pictures – the composers of the music – the competence of the pianist. Even about the fashions my eye could guide me well enough to describe what I'd seen. I did not dwell on my dislike of the crowds – my dependence on Fitz's casual acceptance of so many people in one place – though no doubt Hesketh could tell what I had felt whether I said it or not. But I didn't know what Meredith's job was –

why she was there – in what quasi-official capacity – or any of the personal details which Hesketh seemed to presume I would have divined at first meeting. I could only say that I liked her very much – she was a wild swan, but friendly. If my answers disappointed Hesketh she was still cheerful, only withdrawing to her studio late.

The waters slowly receded as the tide began its reverse flow along the channels – the marsh steamed in the sunshine – midges descended – the mud began to cake on the road. Fitz came slowly along the causeway when it was nearly evening. I had the door open – for some reason – and made out her figure in the distance – jacket over her shoulder – stick under her arm – strolling along some boulevard of her imagination. By the time she reached the yard Hesketh had appeared.

'My dear,' she said swiftly. 'I'm so sorry you couldn't get back to us before, because of the tide – you've had to wait for ages. Kezia was a little worried, but I told her you would manage. Did you have a good time?'

Fitz grinned. She looked terrible – rough hair, dark-socketed eyes, a flush on the cheek-bones – yet simultaneously wonderful – alight. Hesketh again appeared to be trying not to laugh. She drew Fitz in – most unprecedentedly made her a cup of tea. I noticed Fitz seemed unable to speak – although she smiled politely – accepted Hesketh's ministrations gratefully – her silence was otherwise unbroken. She stared into space smiling – occasionally shaking her head like someone stunned with good news. I found this incomprehensibly irritating. I went up to bed early. I was woken by the noise of cork from bottle – heard them talking now downstairs – quietly enough but still audibly in that flimsy house. Fitz was saying, in an almost reverent voice, 'It was pure chance that she was there.'

130

Fitz

Hotter than July. I spread my jacket on the grass for Meredith, stared at her perhaps rudely, at the little curved lines in her face when she smiles, the length of her eyelashes, the colour of her lips. I can still hardly believe she appeared there, like a mirage of longing. She kicked off her shoes and I saw with a curious twist of delight that her toenails were painted shell pink. I've spent so much time trying to imagine being with Meredith again, recalling what she's like, speculating about what she truly feels for me or whether it's the same for her, that I was completely taken aback at actually meeting her. It didn't matter; she talked amusingly, charmingly, though she seemed surprised too. She did not conceal her pleasure at finding me here; she said that she'd only been sent at the last moment to see if the singers would do for another programme (and they wouldn't). Then she added, 'If I'd realised it was anywhere near you, Fitz, I'd have organised it all properly weeks ago, sent a car for you both – I'm terribly vague about geography. Everything seems equally remote when there are no signposts... '

I told her that I'd missed her, more than London.

To Kezia (who was struck dumber than Crambo) Meredith was friendly; after a while Kezia told her she was a swan like one of our known swans, not in the great flock. I thought not everyone would understand this, but Meredith took it as a compliment; she agreed with Kezia that the wild swans wish to be befriended by us. To me her manner was rather more teasing. She laughed at me for telling her she'd be sunburnt, she was so fair; said, 'I do have to be very careful, Fitz.' When a ladybird landed on my collar, she leant forward to make it fly; her hand brushed my face and I smelt her scent for a moment. I wanted nothing but for her to stay flirting with me in the garden like that, sometimes saying my name, but a bell sounded to summon us back indoors.

During the second half of the concert, which was god-awful singing, I could see her all the time, sitting diagonally in front of me to the side of the stage, head bowed. Her hair kept sweeping forward, catching the sun; she hooked it back behind her ear with a childish gesture which I found strangely touching. Once she pushed the hem of her shirt further down inside her skirt waistband, slightly shifting her balance with a unobtrusive movement which almost overset my own stillness. Now she was present, all the uncertainties which have beset me in Saltstreet were dismissed. I remembered the intense voice of her letters, so much said between us already, still so much to say. When she looked at me again, a slow open glance, I knew.

At the end she came over to me very directly.

'Can you stay? There's a party. We're put up at the pub for the night.'

'Kezia?'

'Bring her, of course. There'll be lots of young ones there.'

But Kezia didn't want to, couldn't, pleaded that she had to make Hesketh's supper. I promised her that we wouldn't abandon Hesketh, went back to find Meredith by the stage in the long library.

'I'll have to take her back. She can't go alone.'

'Can you come back? If I get you a driver?'

It meant much to me that she understood, didn't try to make me send Kezia off on her own, or persuade her to stay against her inclination.

'Of course I'll come back, if I have to walk. It might be late.'

'Doesn't matter when.'

The room was quiet now, but she pulled me by the sleeve through a door faced with books, into a tiny room, a dust-smelling priest's hole, within the curved wall, where a miniature staircase led up to the gallery. She told me the way to find her afterwards, where she would be, directions murmured between kisses on my hands, a touch of her soft mouth on my fingers for each instruction. Never any route so well-remembered, although I asked her to tell me again.

The driver commandeered by Meredith was the driver who had first brought me to Saltstreet from the station; to my surprise she remembered me.

'You look better than when I last saw you,' she said familiarly.

Kezia looked at me with interest. We took the pianist and her assistant to the station first, then set off along the coast road where the trees' long evening shadows lay across the road like furrows of floodwater. During the drive towards Saltstreet I let myself fall into a drowsy trance, illuminated by the thought of Meredith; that she, she had arranged everything. But on the return journey, after I'd waved Kezia out of sight along the causeway, I was happy already, as never before. We sped fast along the weaving coast road, empty of other traffic, to get back before dark; I felt the wild sense of being alive, more potently than I knew it existed. That remains with me now, intensely, as though it is a new faculty granted by love.

Crambo

There's a storm every season, there has to be, the sea has to do it, make it all like that, otherwise you might forget what it can be like. It's not the same as the flood tide, when the water comes in and comes in and forgets to stop, rolling in, moving up, until it seems it must never pause, that it will just smoothly cover the marsh, the inland fields, the low hills, the blue hills, until everything is sea everywhere, all directions the same, no inland, no outland, just sea. Storm is different, louder and fiercer and grander than exploding bombs, far more, the waves lob themselves at the ground so hard they burst open and fly up into the air as high as a tree, all spume and foam-spouts, a forest of white frilled trees. You can't walk near the waves, if they sprang on you it would be like a ship crashing over, battering down, crushing. When the great waves like that collide with the land, the ground shudders, the earth shakes underneath the white trees' stamping.

I stand and watch, I love it, I cheer when the highest spouts ring out, egg it on to do more. The smell is crackling, salt-wet lightning, breathing it in makes you want to shout, to dodge in among the waves and ride the water like a sea-person, to be a storm as well. The elements are all mixed up, so the air is heavy with salt water flying in it, and the sea is light with the bubbles of air beaten in, it fizzes as it fans out across the beach, the air shimmers with water-beads pearling it. The sea should be frightening, stir people up, remind them what it can do if it feels like it. The dead sailors down there dance when the storms go rummaging round, rumpling the water up. I love that. The sea only scares me when it's quiet, very still and grey, all the light gone out of it and no bright in the sky, dull cloud, nothing. What if it never changed back, stayed nothing, always? Then I shout at it, bloody old sea, wake up, come back at once, but it doesn't take any notice, it does it when it's ready. A breeze comes across it, or a crack in the clouds, something stirs, and it's living again. It breathes.

During the worst storms, all the inshore lights stay on all night, even up the creek the waves dash over the quay, the splash rattles the door knockers of the houses. There are places where the water comes over the rooftops, waves like a cliff collapsing across the street, and in the morning the boats are all set askew on top of the harbour side where the sea lifted them up and dropped them. I haven't seen that but I know about it, I hear it from the sea. The best one, the best one was a summer storm, not the biggest, the highest ever, but wild, with thunder-claps to make you duck your head quick, long rolls of thunder-mumble to rattle your teeth, and lightning cracking the dark sky-bowl into fissures, streams of lightning rushing down it into the sea, all around. I was very pleased and frightened, dark and flash, dark and flash, the mad sea was wild, yes, alive.

All the others on the beach who try to gain a toehold on my island stay inside when it's like this, keep the lights on, bolt the door. They want to ignore it, pretend it's not there, so it can't get them. Except Kezia, she knows about it, the breakers, the rollers, the storm waves. Maybe Hesketh did too, I don't know, but not the rest of them, not the ones that go out on it, not the ones that sit and watch it. The sea shows them, reminds them about itself, this swell, this source, this force. The seals violently juggled by the waves, the limpets shuddering on their flayed rocks, Crambo benighted on the windy dune top, all must acknowledge it.

After that storm I was on the tideline early, always search in the reeds after the high tides, I find little sea urchins hanging like pods on the green grasses, shells in the lavender, crabs hurrying along the road searching for the sea. Once I saw a big jelly fish caught in a puddle behind the dunes, it had been swept round by the tide and stranded, it breathed drawing its legs in and out, balling up and floating loose, waiting for the sea to come back for it. The seaweed gets caught on the bulrushes, the fishing nets snag on the gateposts. It makes me laugh, the world turned upside-down, fish swimming in the houses, bells ringing under the sea.

I saw Kezia running down the safe path trodden through the wire and the sand to the wet beach, and I wanted to follow her but she was crying, she was running down there to swim and be alone, she didn't like to be with me any more. I don't know why not. I am here, won't go away, won't ever be different, won't want anything else. I got rid of Stevens for her. Trousers next.

All the time Kezia is on the beach, I know Hesketh is looking out, watching us through Her binoculars with Her gun and Her black dog ready. My bones ache under Her gaze.

Meredith

*You caught my imagination the first time I saw you that
evening at the bookshop, silent in the crowd as a prince under
enchantment, perhaps even looking at the books; I can't recall
what they were launching or reading. Was it poetry? You were
in that trousers-and-overcoat out-of-uniform uniform which
all the drivers wear. (I'm sure you never call them 'slacks', do
you?) I saw you as a mythical creature, rare as the unicorn,
solitary, a knight riding alone through a dark wood, some
complex poignance about your solitude, some disinheritance
or enforced disguise endangering your quest. I suppose you
have to have four-o'clock-in-the-morning courage for it, Fitz,
your sort of otherness; I salute you for it. The impression was
only slightly spoilt when Jocelyn tapped you on the shoulder
to show you something in a book – which I couldn't help
presuming was mildly suggestive, if not positively obscene –
and you put your head back to laugh, showing all your teeth,
quite uninhibited. But I cling to the melancholy knight, who
can co-exist with the lounge lizard. I saw that Fitz in action,
too, before we ever spoke; when you laughed like that the
charm shone out of you. All the women liked to touch you,
I noticed, a hand on the elbow, a pat on the shoulder; one
even came up behind you and adjusted your perfectly straight
collar, without a word. You gave in to their ministrations with
a sort of solid resignation which I found very funny, although
I felt a little jealous – you are also a flirt, a performer who
can't resist taking the stage, I observe. I thought loftily about
the women, poor dears haven't the least idea of what their
actions mean, then I looked at you again and thought – some
of 'em are damned sure.*

When Jocelyn finally introduced us (immediately I am

terrified – what if she hadn't? – but she did) you kissed my hand, or perhaps you only behaved as though you had. Fitz, were you a little drunk? I can't remember the words now, can you, which seems strange, but I know we talked about Between the Acts, you recited almost word-perfectly the passage about the swallows: 'The other trees were magnificently straight. They were not regular, but regular enough to suggest columns in a church; in a church without a roof; in an open-air cathedral, a place where swallows darting seemed, by the regularity of the trees, to make a pattern, dancing, like the Russians, only not to music, but to the unheard rhythm of their own wild hearts.' (I copied it out.) We could easily have swept past each other like swallows, calling but not stopping. Did you know then, Fitz? I can't resist asking you again. I knew. It surprised me rather – I have all those years of being a smart worldly young thing to answer to, so I mean the love-at-first-sight lightning-strike, which you so romantically have always expected, was a shock, not the other aspect. Although that was quite startling, too. But I didn't waste any time thinking oh-so-sophisticatedly, 'Oh, that was sexual attraction, how interesting,' before moving on to another party, firmly forgetting it. No, it wasn't like that.

The day after, Sunday, I went to have tea on the houseboat. Mac was late – as ever – so I walked on the river beach, mudlarking. It's shingly there, in fact, not ooze – I expect you recall? Sometimes there's even a patch of perfect white sand, just placed there to take an incised heart and initials. You remember, I'm sure, being taken there sometimes as a child. The embankment walls were as sinister as the granite sides of a pyramid, but above them the sun still shone, the river was crammed with a regatta's worth of boats, the gravel was a treasure trove: clay pipe stems (never the bowls), worn *draughts counters of broken china (always blue and white), mysterious lengths of rusted piping, smooth bricks like half-sucked boiled sweets… I once found half a tile, diagonally split, a design of blue birds on a white ground; I kept that for years. On that Sunday I found nothing, I was thinking of you – how not – if a Roman bronze head or a sword sacrificed to the river had tripped me up, I would probably not have noticed. I conjured you there, playing ducks and drakes, threatening me with slimy objects, raising your lapel high to shelter my cigarette as you proffered your lighter-flame. Why weren't you there? You would have been like that, wouldn't you?*

I thought, we have this one life, now, this one chance. I've already taken some wrong turnings (such an accurate cliché – that awful blank realisation that one is completely lost); the only thing we have is now, I mustn't waste it. It felt like some sort of revelation, standing there on the river bank, wanting you to be there with me. In that situation, that moment of having fallen in love, people are supposed to be uncertain about the future, about whether the love will take wing, is reciprocated, will be happy, if it ever lasts. But I wasn't: I was sublimely resigned to whatever might happen, as long as something did, while there was still time. I suppose it's because of this war; one just thinks 'Let it begin.'

Fitz

Yesterday, I was perched on a tall stool in Hesketh's studio, looking out with her at the panorama of the sea, the beach, Kezia swimming in the distance, Crambo ambling about like a stag beetle in the dunes. My body was still singing so I was distracted from anything else.

'Don't you think Kezia should have fallen in love by now?' Hesketh said, almost apologetically.

'*Kezia*?' (I hadn't been thinking about Kezia.) 'I haven't noticed anything – like that. She seems so very young.'

'At her age, I had been in love many times. But naturally my situation was very different.'

'She didn't seem too pleased by Stevens' declaration.'

Hesketh waved this aside.

'I had hoped you might provide a solution,' she said, with some impatience. 'But you have no idea of how she is, or what she needs.'

'*Me?*'

Hesketh considered me disconcertingly. Her eyes looked almost anemone-purple.

'Of course, quite impossible. But she needs rescuing from here, from me too, probably.'

'She doesn't want to leave here, and certainly not to leave you, Hesketh.'

'No, but she should want to by now, shouldn't she? The grip of the place is too strong. It has her. Which is why I must arrange matters.'

I should perhaps have said conventional things about soon being able to meet people again in an ordinary way, once the war was over, but Hesketh isn't a person to hear platitudes patiently.

'You, Fitz, need to be very careful; she's never met anyone like you before.'

'I have tried to be …'

'I don't mean be discreet about your private life, I mean don't lead Kezia on, since you have nothing to offer her. *Don't kiss her.*'

Stuttering never seems convincing, I've noticed, but I could hardly do anything else.

'Hesketh, that's unfair; I never have, I never *would* …'

'Bear it in mind,' she said austerely, very much like a Victorian papa warning off an ineligible but enthusiastic suitor.

'I shall be gone soon now.'

I went out when I could, feeling obscurely guilty yet outraged, more than ever yearning for London. Although none of the household tasks had yet been done, nor my letters written, I took my swimming towel, ran down to the sea, past the barbed wire, along the path where it snakes across the soft sand through the minefield. Beyond, the wet ribbed seabed sand is safe to wander over, even to run (as I can now, a little awkwardly) to the brink of the sea. Kezia saw me, waved almost shyly. I stripped off my shirt and shorts, kicked off my shoes, waded out until the water was just deep enough to swim in. Floating on her back, Kezia was sleek as a seal; she did not speak to me. I could tell she was upset with me now. I suppose she wants me to be a child still, like her; is disturbed to realise that I'm not.

I swam, working my damaged muscles until they were tired, then floating for the pleasure of the water. When I waded out Kezia was lying in the shallows, scrubbing at her halo of hair with sandy fingers.

'Shall we go out to the wreck?' she said, before I lay down.

'All right.'

(That was something I'd avoided so far; I thought perhaps now it would please her.)

It's a cargo ship, wrecked when it ran inshore to ground on a sandbank, so Kezia once told me. The crew walked ashore, but the cargo had vanished before its owners came to retrieve it, a dull shipment of wood, coal, iron tools. This happened some time in the nineteen-hundreds. Now the ship, looking black against the pale shore, has just its two ends with nothing to connect them but the blank ship-shaped space between, except for one central plug around the stump of a mast. It lies a long way out, completely covered at high tide, only completely revealed at the lowest. The sea has come further in since that stormy night; one day the boathouse will be out on the sandflats too.

It is a long walk; before we were halfway there my leg was aching, shooting pains stabbing up it from my foot. We reached the deep-cut channel which divides the beach at this end, hardly ankle-deep then, crossed it easily. Kezia walked swiftly, her eyes fixed on the wreck, not ignoring me, but not solicitous as usual. The sealbank, out where we usually have to look through the telescope to see seals basking, was close enough now to be able to make them out, lying there like smoothly rounded speckled pebbles.

'Are we going to have time to get back, Kezia?'

'The tide hasn't turned yet. I can feel when it does.'

Up close the wreck seemed to be unexpectedly high, its black sides threatening; a strong instinct enjoined me to avoid it. Perhaps there is still a whiff of human terror caught in its petrified planks, a ghostly shadow of that bad moment when it shuddered onto solid ground. Kezia climbed up the rungs which protruded from the hull like manacle staples;

I followed her more awkwardly. The decks have gone, and inside each hulk-end remnant circuit of dark walls is a blank arena, deep-scoured and curved by the waves' turning in it. It's a place to drown. The hair stood up on my head as I looked down into it. Kezia sat astride the balustrade, cocky, drumming on it with her heels.

'Shall I jump down inside?'

'*No.*'

'Shall we go back now?'

'I think so.'

We went back, as she said, diagonally across the expanse of watermarked sand, with the house gleaming as our beacon, the incoming waves lapping at our heels. I was limping noticeably now: placing my foot down onto the hard sand ridges was increasingly painful with each step. The wavelets which had pursued us overtook, the larger waves which followed them pushed us impatiently along.

'You go ahead,' I said.

'No.'

'It's a good thing we've got our swimming things on. I can always swim in, don't wait for me.'

'Fitz – there's a cross-current here – the channel fills up ahead of us – it gets deep – it isn't safe to swim in from here – even Crambo can't.' I thought she might be going to cry.

'We'd better hurry then.'

Now Kezia came round to my left side, took my arm (although I hardly felt I could lean my weight on her insubstantial frame, too like a moonbeam, as I told her). We hurried. I noticed the waves around us running at curious angles now, the channel ahead shining like a well-filled ditch already. It was waist-deep when we crossed it, crawled up the glutinous bank on the other side. The graphic advance of the water seemed to slow then, caught back by that natural moat, but Kezia still hustled me on. Only when we reached the common tideline did she let me stop. I sank down on the soft shingly slope of the minefield, gripping my leg, groaning, while Kezia knelt beside me, kissed me and held me.

Today, I'm lame again.

Crambo

Slowly, I clean the beach. Stevens stays off it now, and the others, they know now to be very careful. The Crambo paths aren't for them, even if there are ways. *Sand land mine mine.* Pity he only got a fright, I wanted him to vanish, disappear on the air like spray. When I make the noises happen at night, the crash splinters the darkness, fissures of light fly up like sound you can see. It seems louder when everything else is quiet. Nothing should make as much noise as that, so that the silence takes a long time to heal afterwards. A seashell against your ear makes a whispering sound, a wave-song, which is loud enough to say everything. But when I hear those huge crashes I get all excited, I get in a state, I run around laughing and screaming until I can't stop. *Crash splash mash bash.* The moon comes up low, so big she's not light yet, soft disc, only candle-coloured, distant and pale behind the bright explosions. She floats there unreachable, calm, not upset by noises or flashes, not pleased either, beyond. I promise the moon they will all be gone soon, voided, unmade by Crambo. I stare at the moon, eyeball to skyball, to take away the darkness inside me, stop me hearing the terrible noises of the ground breaking.

Calmly, she drenches me in slowness again, quiet runs off me like rain. She rises higher, growing whiter, smaller, infinitely bright. The sea moves up towards her, she gathers the sea up like her long skirts, like a silvery scarf draped across her shoulders she twitches it higher. *Twist mist. Wave slave.* I sing her a quiet song, a lullaby to hush the earth too, smooth it again after the disturbance, bring back the silence and the wholeness from before, before the peace was broken. Let the crabs go back to their holes, the birds to their nests, the fish to their watery furrows, the voles to their sedgy sleep. Let the beach remake itself afresh, even if it has to be destroyed to make it clean again, that's what I sing. It is the best I can do.

Kezia

Nothing was said about Fitz's ordeal – which she gallantly tried to conceal – nobody asked what I had been up to – I had no idea myself. She was stalwartly stoical as ever – even when Hesketh herself applied the long-forgotten lineament – brewed her ditch-teas. The only reparation I could make was to take her letters down to the stile and bring her post back. I resisted looking at the envelopes – there were a lot of them. The weather turned grey – muggy – with thunder in the afternoons – brief rain splashing in few violent gobbets. I felt forlorn – Hesketh was wordlessly reproachful – Fitz was lost to us in a dream.

One such afternoon I walked along the causeway – inland – as far as the church. Time ebbed and flowed there – I remembered first exploring it as a child, when the flint walls were so alien to me. The untidy churchyard was unchanged – crammed with monuments to unknown sailors found drowned – memorials to wrecks which had gone down with the loss of all hands – always with the ship carved in miniature on the stone – not sombre but toylike. Inside there were whole walls devoted to lists of names of the dead claimed by the sea – lighthouse keepers – fishermen – unwary holidaymakers – sailors and naval men – and (on a magnificently lettered board with much space prudently left ready to be filled) the great roll of honour for the lifeboat crews who had 'gone out in all weathers to prevent loss of life'. As a child I had cried over them – their courage – their inevitable end – and swiftly forgotten them. Now the church door was locked – a notice pinned on it about services in other churches. I waited in the damp stone-smelling porch while the lavish rain spattered down as vehemently as the seagulls' sudden shit-showers.

That first day – freshly landed there – the door was open. I went confidently in – was disconcerted by the stark church interior – no holy water – no votive candle pyramids – no altarpieces – no dark glitter. It was just melancholy peeling whitewash – an achingly sad English grey light – an afternoon commemorating nothing but emptiness. I wandered about – floating in the silence – saw a curious display on the altar steps – some foreign ritual. There were several large baskets full of fruit or vegetables of unlikely size – an attractively displayed wheatsheaf – other piles of foodstuffs – even tins. I examined this charitable offering judiciously. There were plenty of tins in the store cupboard at the boathouse, but we had no fresh food as yet. I took a fine marrow – apples – pears – onions – potatoes – a dozen eggs – all the large mushrooms seductively arranged in a moss nest (because I thought they would not last). I carried it all back in a sack which had covered the carpet under the marrows. Hesketh was delighted.

As I sat remembering all this – Crambo darted into the porch like a swallow sweeping in to its nest. I sprang up to go out just as swiftly but he caught at my hand.

'Kezia,' he said in his guttural loose voice so it sounded like *Keshar* – 'Why won't you stay with me?' I understood what he said well enough even when he only spoke half-words.

'I don't *trust* you,' I said – pulled free of him – walked out into the rain – back along the reed-fringed road to the causeway – where the disturbed water winked and leered at me through the gaps in the rotted planking.

From the church knoll behind me came a Crambo litany – bellowed back with all the vehemence I had spat at him.

'*Trust must lust crust dust.*'

The last word pleased him most – even when I was back

indoors I could still hear him crooning – ululating – DUST DUST DUST.

Now they didn't ring the church bells any more I never knew which day was Sunday – it didn't make any difference anyway. On Sundays – heartrendingly – Hesketh sometimes liked to make a little festival, talk about the old days, wear one of her glamorous dresses. Fitz was good about this. I did what I could with the food – this time it was smoked mussels out of a rather mature tin, with a newer tin of mushy peas and some macaroni. Fitz opened a bottle of wine, listening over her shoulder to Hesketh's recounting some episode of past glories – asked who Tony was – perhaps to prove she was paying attention – Hesketh tended to punctuate her anecdotes with exhortations to concentrate.

'Who's Tony? Anthony! Wicked Antonio, Kezia's father – surely I said so before?' Something in Hesketh's offhand manner contrasted so strangely with her previous distress that I was suddenly afraid.

'You wouldn't go back to him would you?' I burst out childishly.

Hesketh stared at me for a moment – mouth theatrically widened.

'What?' she cried, 'dismiss my genius? Don't you know, chick, I could never work with him? All my painting, my summoning, my arts, have flourished since we came here, since he exiled us. I shall never relinquish my powers; I'd rather drown myself.'

'Good,' I said.

I saw Fitz watching us both with such a tender expression – strong sympathy and encouragement combined – and saw Hesketh through her eyes – damaged yet still precious – the silver clock which no longer keeps good time but on occasion memorably chimes.

Then Fitz said – 'So there are compensations for coming here?'

'Oh, great ones. The greatest. But it was still the loss of a great love.'

I was baffled by her simultaneous relief and regret. Later, there were more conversations about love – I asked Hesketh about what it meant – that soldier being 'in love' with me – she hesitated a long time before answering.

'I'm sure he thinks he is; he seems an almost dauntingly sincere young man. (Though we haven't been troubled by him recently, have we? I suppose we must thank Crambo for that.) But since you've never properly spoken to him, his idea of you perhaps may not be very real, may be more of an imagined person, a fantasy. What do you think?'

'I think it's ridiculous.'

She sighed – laughed – agreed.

This gave me an idea. I went to find Fitz who was folded up into her window seat reading – interrupted her brutally.

'Are you in love with Meredith?'

'I am,' she said, in her frank way.

'How long have you known her? Do you *know* her?'

Fitz put down her book – stared out of the window – narrowed her eyes.

'Well – I've known her about a year, nearly. We were introduced by a friend of mine who works in a bookshop, because we kept wanting the same books, so she thought we'd get on. But the war made things difficult, then I got hurt, sent away. I am starting to know her now, in one way; in another way as soon as we first met I recognised her, as though I already knew her very well. But also, I have an odd feeling

I can never know her enough, or not as much as I'd like to.'

'I see,' I said – but I didn't.

Fitz considered the view again – then told me – in a measured way – what had happened to her family – as though it somehow explained everything about why she loved Meredith. So many people – she said – had died or vanished or been lost in some dark place – it was nothing unusual – except that it had happened to her. Her grandfather had been wounded in Spain – he was a pacifist but he went with a Quaker ambulance as a stretcher bearer. Fitz seemed to think that this had been a lucky outcome for him – heroism within his principles – perhaps achieved at the expense of his relations? Her mother had gone to Spain – found him recovering in hospital – stayed on working for the Red Cross as a volunteer until he was well enough to come home. After he came back, he died quite soon – the Fascists had won in Spain by then – Fitz's mother went back to France to work with the refugees from Spain who were in camps there. Fitz wanted to help too – but she was at university – her mother wanted her to finish there first – she only went once during the holidays.

'It was a weird experience,' she said, with the animation she always showed talking about other places. 'There were so many people there, in despair really, then so many whose whole job was to help them, all those Quakers who do nothing else, an odd mixture of idealism and institutionalised charity. It was chaos as well. My ma spent all day interpreting for the people who were trying to get permits to go on. I ended up giving puppet shows for all the kids who'd escaped. Everyone was shell-shocked, hungry, exiled, but at least they were there.'

I thought that she'd been doing this when she was younger

than me; she had entertained tents full of orphans, and I'd never met one. When the war came some of the people stayed on in France when the others were evacuated – for a while they were in the unoccupied part of France – then they had to leave there as well – Fitz explained it all but she needed a map really to make me understand. Her mother got to Lisbon – in Portugal – with a man she'd lived with in France, I gathered – where they were stranded. Letters and cards used to come quite often – but then irregularly – now there haven't been any for a long while.

'There are numberless organisations which reunite the people who have lost each other because of this war,' Fitz said, almost grimly. 'All of them know where to find me, who I'm looking for. It can't be much longer. I know she'll be trying to get home, too.'

Years ago this had happened – when I was a child still – before the war came here. So Fitz had been a student – not much older than I was now – alone in her house – with her people absent – silent – with the hope they might come back. All the time since she had never stopped believing that she would meet them again one day – it frightened me to think what might happen if she was wrong. I thought of how strong she was – yet not hardened – how she had made herself alone – that only someone in particular could understand even a part of what she knew.

Meredith

The house is still just as you said. It's so quiet down the alley, grass growing between the cobbles, the trains' slow drumroll sounds distant even in the still air – a companionable noise for a child's bedtime. It's only a bus ride away. No wonder you feel sad about it, my dear, it's a dolls' house; one imagines the Two Bad Mice living there. I looked over the wall into the garden as directed, squinted through the front shutters and saw all the panelling inside: shutters, wainscot, tiny stairs in a cupboard, the partition, the fireplace. It must have been like living inside an inlaid box, delightful for a child – a Georgian ribbon-shop once, perhaps? You must tell me its history one day, why it remains there, how your grandparents came to have it. (We have so much to talk about.) It will survive, I'm sure; it looks solid enough to outlast us all. One hears these tales of bomb-shaken buildings suddenly collapsing, like a person fainting hours after their shock, but not so long after, when everything around still stands firm. A pity all the window-glass has gone; I imagine it as that bottle glass, bubble-bearing and water-marked as a slice of the sea itself. But it's only the glass. Admittedly the restoration will be an undertaking, but such things are possible again now; one sees repair teams at work all over London. The house looks weatherproof, safe enough, in hibernation for the time being.

I understood what you said about the guilty relief of losing possessions, those drowning-stones, which alternates with intense distress about one's weightlessness. Only yesterday, a woman at work told me that she was secretly delighted to have discarded all the china which she'd inherited, the furniture she'd dutifully polished while disliking it, the hideous Victoriana which had accumulated, been bequeathed

153

or presented. (She plans to start again uncluttered with things in her own taste: pale wood, Scandinavian style!) I don't suggest that your loss of precious remembrances is comparable to her liberation, but the true sense of those things will never be lost to you, Fitz: you are their crucible. Objects themselves may carry the presence or the blessing of their owner, but not so much as the people they loved. No photograph can compare with looking in the mirror – but perhaps it's too soon for you to feel this, not yet.

What I would say to you, with the effrontery of absolute truth, is that home is here. No house could shelter either of us as well as a coat over our heads in the rain, if we were in the street together. (I am not stating the literal facts of bricks and mortar; we have my flat over the empty studio, a roof above.) To make a place for you which will give you a sense of home, like that you lost so long ago but fit for you as you are now, I will spread a picnic rug, open an umbrella; weave willow branches together, daub them with London clay; set up a silken pavilion or a carpet-hung tartar tent; find a cave near a spring with a fire-stone or an island in a lake with a hermitage; buy a caravan with an old slow horse and a cookpot swinging or a narrowboat with windowboxes and a tin stove-pipe. Whatever we need, we'll make up – but you know that; your heart has come home already.

Fitz

Since Crambo has taken to blowing up the mines on the foreshore (narrowly missing poor Stevens, whose nerves have certainly not yet recovered) our neighbours are not in evidence very much. This is convenient, even if we cannot condone the method. Crambo is too clearly capable of murder, but Stevens prefers to think 'the accident' was a result of misjudged high spirits rather than (very) diminished responsibility. But I notice he doesn't turn his back on Crambo any more if they ever meet on the causeway; none of the soldiers swim – the beach is delightfully free of their presence. We have re-possessed it, at ease on the sand with Crambo's goodwill; it is Kezia's own again. The paths through the minefield grow wider; before long the coast will be clear. Even when Crambo goes berserk, detonating a couple more of the evil devices every night, we merely laugh.

Stevens still looks as though he's in recovery from some fearful Biblical plague, his skin a shale of shallow scabs and red abrasions, his twitches pronounced. If we encounter him on the road, apart from the speech-impediment which has flown into his mouth with half the beach, he has little to say, but I suspect he misses Crambo. It won't be long before they are cronies again, even if Stevens has the wit to stay wary. The moment after the explosion, when he appeared on the doorstep as a pebbledashed statue, will recur in our satirical nightmares. (As the *Commendatore* Stevens wasn't entirely convincing.) Now, I wonder how we all knew immediately what had happened, united to christen it an accident, gave him whisky for the shock, admonished him on the danger of walking through a minefield for a swim. Hesketh assured him magnanimously that we would say nothing about it, since we had no wish to get him into serious trouble; we all promised our silence.

Now, Kezia points out that if Crambo had killed Stevens, or as I hastily rephrased it, if Stevens had died as a result of Crambo's mischief, there would have been police, trials, prison for Crambo, for ever, if not worse. I assured her that no court, even in wartime, could hang Crambo, but privately I'm not so sure.

'It would kill him anyway,' she said with conviction. 'If he ever left here, he couldn't survive. He can't bear to be inside at all, but it's more than that. This is his place.'

'Do you think he is actually trying to clear the mines off the beach? Or does he just like the effect they make? Or both, perhaps?'

Dully, from far along the beach by the western outflow, came the sand-blasting thunder which is now Crambo's calling card, followed by the drifting Guy Fawkes' Night scent of gunpowder.

'He really must stop doing that,' Kezia said, quite crossly for her.

While I waited one day last week by the stile while Mrs Dews searched for our parcels in the van, I glanced at her newspaper. Now I can't rid my thoughts of what I've seen. Sometimes when I walk I can hardly understand where I am, for thinking of all that – working is better. When I'm with Kezia or Hesketh, I am so relieved they don't know; I wish they could never find out. Some of these things are unbearable, yet there they are in black and white, print and picture. Beside them are the stories of rescue, reunion, liberation, miraculous survival.

This morning early I went out, on my old cigarette excuse;

it was going to be a fine day. I reached the collapsing fence which separated the barren thistle-patch from the churchyard, rested my forehead on the topmost wooden fence-strut. It was dry, powdery, riven, scentless as an old bone. I remembered the rabbit's skeleton we had seen, arched on a tump of moss like a precious relic on a green cushion. Clean as a sea-stripped shell, intricate, strangely beautiful, its complex pattern a fretwork of whittled twigs, a corn doll, a musical instrument – it was an image to contemplate unflinching. Compared to the rest, the other anguish, it was nothing at all, for all its grim presence: it was only death.

When I opened my eyes, straightened up, the mark of the wood ingrained on my forehead, the view had altered. With a rustling clipping noise, like nothing but themselves, a flock of goldfinches had settled on the thistles. The new sun caught their blazons of red on the head, their black bandannas, their bright yellow capes. Clumps of thistledown drifted about, less delicate than the birds' impatient beaks, while the sound of their thin joyous cries was the imagined voice of jewels darting. So fragile, so vivid among the thorns, they fed for a few moments then rose up in a coloured cloud, were gone. It was nothing but chance to have witnessed their descent, like an impersonal blessing flashing down to gild a random corner of this troubled world.

Kezia

Hesketh painted me – often – once in a strange double portrait with Crambo when we were children – which she said it would be too obvious to call *Beauty and the Beast* – also unnecessarily rude to him. In the days when I had Rapunzel she painted me doing it up – my backview reflected in the dressing table mirror – my face half-hidden as I twisted to see the plait behind me. Now I had cut it off, she started to paint me short-haired – a fierce mermaid – bare above the waist. It was a green-hued picture – aquamarine, verdigris, celadon – never finished – abandoned on the easel. The background was a pattern which never became clear – apparently another looking-glass.

This was a curious light-effect which we observed sometimes on the beach – rarely – when the sun was low, white, wintery. If the flat sand was thinly slicked with water – wet uniformly – the sheen on it almost blinded us – a sheet of mirror glass lay utterly flat in every direction – a looking burning-glass. Once I saw this sheer silver-white expanse spotted with tiny clots of shadow in a random neat pattern. The polka dots were worm-casts – in their millions – coil pyramids extruded from the sand – breaking the mirror's smooth reflection like flaking age-spots on an old pier glass – endlessly repeated. Eye-searing – yet impossible not to stare at – this was the infinite background which Hesketh started to conjure for me.

When I walked on the mirror beach once with Fitz, she kept doubling over to stare at herself in it – a stertorous Narcissus – exclaiming with glee at her distorted appearance. I glanced down to meet her upside-down reflection – unfamiliar – head cocked sideways like a robin staring at its double in a puddle.

The sky slid swiftly past beneath our feet. Fitz held out her hand – palm downwards, fingers stretched – bent lower until the touched image vanished with a splash – extinguished through the looking glass.

'Why is it so fascinating outside?' she demanded. 'I don't play with looking glasses indoors. Imagine – before there were mirrors – if this was the only way you could see yourself. Or in a still pool.'

'Or a polished pan, or a spoon-bowl.'

'Or as a shadow on the sand.'

I didn't say 'as Crambo does' – I watched Fitz's visual experiments until she said – 'But everything seems different here, doesn't it?'

Crambo

The lizard's tail twitch on the sand, the grains which trickle down within its footprint, the bird's claw scratching on the dried ground scraping out its shallow nest, sounds I hear. At night I could not sleep for noise, beetles' feet rasp on grass, quills and reeds forever click and jostle, the mudbanks creak and pop air out of their pockets. When rain fell, each drop was a sounding-stone in the well of my head, a watery bell. The blasts moved the stone away for a while from the echoing entrance to my ear. The sea sang all the time, I realised – not only the loud song I'd always known, when it banged all along the shore clapping wave on stone, but other tunes as well: rattle of retreat, clip of foam-spatter, crackle of bubbles abandoned on sand. What was muffled became clear.

Sometimes I thought I would go mad, hearing everything so near. At night I heard the seals stir in their heaps on the bank, flippers slapped, whiskers bristled, eyewhites rolled in the moonlight, heard the soldiers stifled in their bunks, scratch, belch, lurch. I could hear my mother's house creak like a gutted boat-carcase in a gale, even the stones of it sealed in their silence hummed in the gusts of our pain. Nothing is ever quiet, nothing is ever still, the perpetual motion makes perpetual music, too much to hear too much to bear.

It was ecstasy, but also fear.

Meredith

*I understand what you say about your people there, your
refugee-family; they took you in, welcomed you, adopted you
– can you now abandon them? It's a part of your character,
your natural pietas, to consider that. There are those who
have made life-friendships with their hosts, and those who
heartily wish never to see them again. You of course belong to
the category who will be exchanging Christmas cards at the
millennium, who will repay their hospitality a hundredfold.
I know it was lucky for you that you went there – shall we
say fated? – but they were fortunate too, won't be counting
the spoons or fumigating the blankets.*

*Perhaps you should think of your inevitable departure
as you think of your play: merely a problem of characters,
motivation, right moves. Archetypes as you all are; you are
the handsome stranger. It is your task to be the catalyst, to
ride away down the road so that they know there is a way
along which to go. I don't think you can fetch them with you
until they're ready to leave, which is only after their situation
alters, as it must. That's the difficulty, isn't it, with this last
Tempest of yours? Even if the island seems like home, they
are really all in exile. It's only a temporary refuge. They have
to go there to find themselves, then having done so, return to
the starting-point. Some change of heart must take place for
them to come back to us; time must pass to bring this about,
the scene must alter. So you have your task too.*

IV

Fitz

When I write to Meredith we talk about the war being over, about being together, going on holiday to Italy perhaps, or Paris. Solid dreams. I imagine a future, a love affair in a city, happy work, living perhaps together, at least near each other. I hope for things which I dare not yet ask Meredith, then in her letters she fearlessly voices them. She tells me about myself, too. There is a practical element to all this; plans as well as resolutions. As I re-read the letter from Meredith which, of all her testaments to me, is the one I treasure most, the song of homecoming to her in safety, I know it is true. I will discard what I do not need to take with me, as the hermit crab in order to grow must shed the shell which was once haven, dare to ride out soft sans carapace, find another shelter suited to its new state. I know myself healed, as much as any of us may be from our deep or surface wounds; it is time to adventure.

So I have written to old Brad to thank her for organising such a successful convalescence, while politely explaining that I'm returning to London with or without permission. She may not even pretend to be angry; if I can drive, she will be pleased to see me. It was not even difficult to speak to Hesketh about leaving; she just agreed that it was time for me to go, now I am so much better. I asked my friend Jocelyn if I could come back to stay in the flat next week, just for a while, if I need to, but then I wrote to Meredith again, with other suggestions. Meredith replied to me *Yes. To everything.*

Now I have made the arrangements, I can only wait. On the appointed day a car will collect me, take me to the station, to the train back to London, my proper realm, my theatre of operations. Meredith will meet me, we'll go back to her flat together, afterwards go out to a restaurant with candles in bottles on the check-clothed tables. There will be plane trees, pavements, lamp-posts, battered enamel street names, everywhere those blessed, beloved signs for the Underground. I try to hide my delight from my hosts; it seems hardly decent. After all, I am not pleased to be leaving them, only to be going home.

I am conscious of these last days in Saltstreet dawdling to their close unlamented as any school term, tour of duty, prison sentence. Perhaps the ending of any marked measure of time, even a banishment, might bring about a revulsion of feeling, a last-minute nostalgia before the long-looked-forward-to happy ending. But for me there is only the admission, lightly made, that we will all miss each other, of course. Hesketh may occasionally regret not being able to cadge my cigarettes, or reminisce to a new audience; Kezia will miss my predictable knight's move at chess, my visible protection on her walks. But she is the same as ever, a sea-green incorruptible; she shuns the soldiers still. I realise neither of them will ever change, any more than they expect anyone else to alter. (Neither of them has noticed that I'm not smoking any more.)

The holiday snaps I shall take away with me are all (conveniently enough) pictures that make me smile to remember them: the soldiers vainly trying to play football on the beach despite Crambo's hysterical interventions as he relentlessly followed the ball back and forth, barking, or occasionally took possession of it to race off towards the sea; the bead-eyed crab which reared up at my feet waving its larger claw – perhaps three inches high – so fiercely that I jumped back, with a yell. I recall putting a shell in my pocket for its beauty, a spiral cone narwhal miniature, only to feel hours later as I sat at supper something move against me, twisting at my side, so that I had to explore my coat with shrinking fingers which brushed against scaly hermit-legs vaguely waving. Kezia went out laughing in the darkness to restore the kidnapped creature to its element, perhaps outraged but unharmed. After that I checked more carefully for signs of prior occupation, having a certain fellow feeling for that displaced thing.

I intend to leave behind at Saltstreet my limp (except for the ghost of it which may still haunt me when I'm tired), also the chorus which used to sing perpetually in my head of loss. There will be other phrases to repeat now, other charms of words to touch for luck. So it is impossible to regret being sent here – who could wish for better luck than that? – but it is time to go. I want life, the sign it made to us from the sea, the reminder to be ready to leap onto the bus-platform, to seize the rail as it speeds by.

Kezia

When she told us the news that she was leaving at last, Fitz said a strangely heartfelt thank you. It almost seemed as though she were grateful to us for making her better – though that would surely have happened anyway – perhaps she was sorry for us having to remain here – or perhaps she thought we would regret her. I found it hard to imagine Saltstreet without her again – or to remember what it had been like in her absence. Afterwards, I dreamt that I went to Fitz – told her that I would go with her to London – she just nodded – looked at me – said, 'What about Hesketh?'

I said, 'I think she wants me to go' – but even as I said it in the dream I wasn't sure it was true.

When I came downstairs – although there was no one about – I felt awkward somehow – confused by my meaningless dreams. I looked out at the day – at the marsh breath stirring its short fleece. On the step was a box – I thought it was a nest for a moment – made of green twigs – almost a basket except for the covering leaves. Before – in the old days – Crambo always left his gifts on the beach side of the house – but I knew this was from him. I opened it – the lid fitted very neatly – inside was a sort of necklace – a nameless Crambo creation – absolutely beautiful. There were large pearls in uneven shapes but matched sizes – discs of mother-of-pearl or opaline shell – lumps of amber polished smooth as cobbles – ivory cubes incised with sea-insignia. The string he'd used was the dark blue waxed twine – oily and heavy – with which they make the very fine almost invisible nets. It was strange – unlike anything else – the barbaric jewellery a royal sea-creature might wear – yet it was unique in Crambo's repertory of tributes. For the first time he had considered what I would like – what would suit me – within the range of his imagination. It was not the neckpiece of a child or a chattel – it was a chain of office from the ocean. I took it as a peace-offering.

That morning – the day before the day Fitz was leaving – I went for a walk alone – looking for Crambo – and of course met Stevens. I think they kept a lookout inland – ignored the sea – for he always seemed to appear like magic whenever I went out. He still looked terrible. Since that time when we had to give him first aid – whisky – insisted that Crambo had just been playing – it was impossible for me to ignore him. I didn't mind him so much now – though I would still much rather have been without him – but I thought it wasn't very safe for him to intercept me. The Burtons had gone – vanished overnight as gypsies are meant to – and now I missed their flamboyant presence (for several reasons).

'Where's Crambo?' I asked meaningfully – he looked nervously about – stuttered.

'He's going to blow himself up one of these days.'

'Well, nobody asked his permission to put those horrible things there in his place, his only place. He's just tidying them up.'

'It isn't his job to be a one-man bomb disposal squad!'

I presumed this was a joke – laughed – to my dismay tears sprang into his red-rimmed eyes.

'Kezia – why don't you like me?'

'I don't *know* you,' I said in a fair imitation of Fitz's forthright manner.

'You're in love with someone else.'

I fled. If I could have disappeared in a sea mist I would have disintegrated gladly – drifted off over the marsh and away. As it was I just ran – as I had in the old days – I was soon gone from him – too far to answer. I could still see him standing abandoned on the causeway – he took his hat off to scratch his head – as I stifled a queasy rise of compunction I thought – is there no getting away from this, even here?

When I ran into the yard there was Fitz – with a letter in her hand. I realised I had never seen her cry before – not like this. Hesketh was beside her – she waved at me through the tears.

'It's from her mother,' she cried, 'from Alonsa, in Lisbon. She's well. They'll be able to come home soon.'

I put my arms round them both – wept too – knew that everything was simple.

Crambo

Kezia sometimes wears the sea-rope I made for her. *Pearl girl.*
Water daughter. She could walk on the waves in that one, if
she wanted to. She said thank you to me, found me outside
specially to say it, but I don't need that, it doesn't matter. It
was for her. All the things which come to the beach are there
for us, we can have them. *Earth birth. Sea me.* I saved the
things for a long time to make that one for her, looked in all
the special places, found them and kept them for later. It was
like when I make the things for the sea, it likes it. *Beach teach
reach each.* She understood what it meant, though, she came
on her own. Hesketh didn't set the black dog on me. Even
when things go wrong, you can make them better sometimes.

After that I tried to tell Stevens about Kezia when he went
to talk to her again, to say you mustn't touch her, like the
moon, you must dance for her, sing to her, make her things,
then have the fierce pleasure if she likes it. But when he saw
me he ran away, and I remembered about not telling any of
them my secrets. I shouted my new Crambos at him over the
marsh, but he didn't listen, I don't know why.

That was the day, that day, when all the ladybirds came
out in their clicking clouds, a flush on the marsh, a scarlet
ribbon edge to the sea. Up close the little bright beads are
like freckled pearls, only red, shiny as glass shards rubbed
round. *Bright flight. Bead seed.* Often when they come out
there are many, so many they might be raindrops dotted on
the road, but that time there were more. After a minute I
had a collar of them, a crown, little beetle-drifts in the folds
of my clothes, jewel buttons all over. It made me laugh, it
tickled, but I didn't want to hurt them by standing, although

there are so many, so the round bodies splay flat, blood-drop shape. So I lay still, I watched them. In the wintertime you sometimes find them, all safe asleep in a crowd like the seals, they make a red lining in some dry crack, holly berries all crammed together in a pod waiting for the warm, when they can fly again.

I stayed there all afternoon, draped in my scarlet pennants, and all the time I could hear them in the boathouse, laughing.

Meredith

Yes. To everything. O Fitz, we can start our life at last, at once. I want the curious angle you make with your elbow as you pull the cork out of a bottle, or the way you look up from your book with your eyes still distant, to be as familiar to me as my own body, but still as romantic as a swanherd's counting song. The discovery of this new world, then the mapping of it, exploring the different landscapes and experiencing its weathers, tending it, living in it as one lives in a beloved place which roots in the heart – this is the future.

I imagine – as you can no doubt guess – many things which in our time together we might do. I think not only of this bedroom, where the sun wakes me every morning through some chink left in these rigid tapestry curtains and a little later, after I've reached for my notebook, shows me the old apple tree in the yard upsidedown on the ceiling in miniature or strikes rainbow fragments off the cut-glass doorknobs. (You have been here often already; I see you cautiously lowering yourself onto the clothes-covered basket chair, or balancing highwire-wise on the bed to examine the books on the top shelf, or hanging your trousers on the hook behind the door. These thoughts can lead to others more disturbing to my equilibrium, more unutterable as yet ...) Delightful as all this is, I think also of the empty room downstairs, of any room which we can call our own, where the quiet throbs with concentration, the flow of making whatever we may make pours down on us like solace, the blessing of work drops gentle as dew, so that when we raise our heads, meet each other's eyes, we are together in that other place.

Yesterday I went downstairs to that long-abandoned work room, opened the tall windows out onto the yard, examined the floorboards, the stove, thought is it light enough, warm enough, could Fitz here chisel, carve, knot, loop, paint, sew, do whatever it is she needs to do to create her microcosmos? Before I could decide, the answer came to me that you would damn well do your work in any corner if you felt like it, any cupboard could be your studio if need be – you could crouch over the kitchen bench while I wrote on a board on my knees. The luxury of sacred spaces purposed for nothing else is what one wants, naturally, but it doesn't have to be so. Wordsmith, playmaker, whatever our work we will always make a place and space to do it, since we have the intense luck to be given the chance. I think the downstairs room might do very well as a workshop for temporary worlds.

Everyone keeps telling me that civilisation lies in ashes, our culture is over or in its last throes, with worse, worse things – at which I look pained or apprehensive. But inside I have a flame of hope, of happiness, turned down low at the moment but ready to flare. Feasting in the ruins, writing at night even while we know the barbarians are burning books, singing against the wind – what else have we ever done? We can have our time, even while we do what has to be done, inherit what's left of the earth. Since we still live, we'll live more intensely, with more awareness, not forgetting what has happened but resolving that since we must live in its shadow, we will live brightly. I do believe in the ultimate victory of the musicians playing in the camps, the women singing a lullaby to the doomed children – they transcend everything else. It won't take us that sort of courage to do our work, put a grain of sand in the scales, but in this all-containing world where everything matters, we'll do what we can.

This reminds me of a poem I once wrote – indeed it was printed in your favourite Time and Tide, *so you may have read it – on the poignance, really, of the quote 'The lyf so short, the craft so long to lerne'. Who hasn't felt like that, whether about their cookery or composing? Then somebody wrote to me, an elderly writer, who said that it was a mistranslation – or rather misunderstanding – of 'Ars longa, vita brevis'; she suggested the rendering, 'Our art outlasts our own short life'. (Possibly I should have taken more notice in Latin at school, but Chaucer was obviously equally vague about it – or preferred the sadness of the brief life?) She's dead now, but her books still breathe. Of course, both versions of the tag are true; life is too short, but there is that almost-consolation in the way some things we make, even if they last as briefly as a flame, survive us ...*

Fitz

The whale was small as whales go, only about as long as the boathouse. It lay aslant the waterline, not straight on, as though it had run aground while trying to turn. Everything else on the beach was right-angled to the tide line, neatly. What seemed extraordinary was the life trembling within something of a scale which could, surely, only be inanimate. Its vastness, like an elephant's, seemed to envelop some paradox of fragility. Its skin was a delicate dark violet-grey, like a spring storm cloud; when I touched it a tremor ran across the whole surface. It felt not like one of the dry frogs Kezia liked to pick up, nor yet like a fish, but strangely like a cold human swimmer, or exactly as the seals felt when they swam beside us.

The sea was nothing but a high wave on the horizon, receded to its furthermost perhaps, or not yet turned. So the whale had been there a long time already; I thought it was as good as dead, the water would not return for so long. I hoped helplessly that Kezia might not see it yet. We once found a small dolphin, an infant of perhaps two feet long, arched on the sand as though it had leapt out of life, and she wept bitterly over it. The thought of the dolphin, drowned (we thought), reminded me that the whale after all breathed air like us, would not suffocate in this element, might survive, might refloat.

'Kezia!' I shouted, like all the others who called on her without answer. 'Kezia!'

She came. She ran down the safe path, over the wet ribbed sand, straight to me where I waited with my strange catch.

'O Fitz,' she said, 'she's so beautiful.'

'Has the tide turned yet?'

'I don't feel that it has, quite. Can she keep alive?'

'I don't know. Should we try to wet her down, do you think?'

'Yes – fetch water – get Hesketh.'

I left Kezia squatting by the whale's head, crooning whatever words she thought might comfort Leviathan. At the front of the house I met Hesketh fetching out what vessels she had for water-carrying: bucket, watering-can, enamel bread-bin, emptied coal-scuttle, tin pitcher.

'The sea is so far away, Hesketh…'

'We'll get water from the creek. It's brackish, but salty enough. I'll call Crambo too. But Fitz, bring the gun.'

She made off down the path, pails clashing, her hair streaming out behind her. (There had been some bad days, but now she is imperial again.) I slid the rifle up out of the umbrella stand, took a handful of bullets from the fruit bowl. I very much hoped Hesketh didn't imagine that we could use it to end the whale's ordeal. On my way after her, I saw Crambo hovering in the dunes, his hurpling a mirror to my lopsided stride which doubtless looked very comic. When I approached he hopped backwards like some periwigged exquisite retreating in a courtly pavane.

'Crambo, didn't you hear Hesketh call you? We need you, please help us.'

At this, he followed me down towards the tide plain, where the whale's bulk lay as oddly as another wreck. It did not occur to me, in my distraction, that he might play the same game that he had with Stevens, and he didn't. The four of us stood, looked at the creature, at each other.

'Oh – the tide is turning,' Kezia said. Hesketh looked at her, benevolent.

'It will be up here in a few hours. If she survives until then,

174

we might be able to send her out again.'

'Fish.'

'It isn't a fish, Crambo, it's a whale.'

'*Fish dish wish…*' Agitation made his voice violently guttural.

'What's he saying, Kezia? I can't understand.'

'The fishermen would eat it, if anyone from the village saw it here.'

Obviously, he was right. They would come down from the quay with cleavers, nets, wooden fish crates – the beach would be awash with mammal blood. We were all hungry, after all.

'What about the soldiers?' I asked grimly.

Fleetingly, we imagined soldiers and fishers fighting it out on the beach, nets and cleavers against bayonets and rifles, in some grotesque gladiatorial struggle. (My money would certainly be on the netsmen.)

'No,' said Hesketh calmly. 'I don't think the Templetons or Mr Bell would be interested in whale meat; they don't even take seals any more, too busy with lobster. Anyway, they never come along here now because of the mines. We have Crambo to help us with that, too.'

He nodded, picked up a stone.

So we ferried water from the creek – not where the freshet ran across the sand in a spread fan, but higher up where its deep channel was cut through cliffs of shingle. When I poured my first watering can full over the whale's side it was like a teaspoonful of liquid on a hillside, which ran straight off. After an hour of toil there was a slight damp patch on the sand around the whale, a shallow puddle defining its outline. The sea looked no nearer, but I remembered the speed with which it ran in when we were racing it back from the wreck.

Kezia

The water-carrying slowed after an hour or so – Fitz bore the brunt of it – labouring back and forth with the heavy burdens – never pausing but steadily, steadily moving to and fro. Crambo worked too – but not for him the dogged repeat of the plough turn – he scuttled wildly about with great outbursts of effort – interspersed with dawdling – singing – brief disappearances. Donkey-work, Fitz called it – happily. Once the whale twitched her tail – enough to make us all leap back – and sometimes her skin quivered slightly.

'We can't keep this up for much longer,' I said – I was thinking of Fitz's revived limp after our walk to the wreck.

Everyone looked at the water approaching – the blue line advancing from the horizon with the precision of a mathematical diagram. It was still far away. The whale – silent in voice – made a sort of clacking noise with her tongue – a stirring of the mouth. Hesketh put her hand on the great forehead – like a woman touching a standing stone – bowed her head a little.

'Come now,' she said, 'we need the waves here early, a spring tide, a surge, a following wind.'

She raised her head to look up at the clouds seething above us in white and grey swathes like the geese-skeins' weaving.

'Let me paint these as rain clouds,' she said.

Fitz sank down on a stone – folded up tightly – with the gun upright in her arms – like a forlorn lookout. I crouched down at Hesketh's feet – whispering to the whale – stories of wet and escape. Crambo had vanished. It was cold – a sharp wind blowing – time was slower than the tide – suspended between ebb and flow. Fitz shouted – a warning sound – pointed out to sea. We looked at what she had seen, and

176

Hesketh smiled. A dark pillar – distinct as a smoke signal – rose from the horizon a little to the west of us and even as we first saw it, came nearer. The incoming wind whisked everything loose on the beach briskly before it – bowling rough baskets of dried weed and sea-rubbish up from the tideline. Sand stung our skins. The storm column was nearly upon us – darkness and chill in advance – then a thick wall of rain – like no rain we ever saw except in the extreme weathers which came sometimes with the highest floodtide.

As it struck, I ran to take shelter in the lee of the whale, who shuddered and stirred. It was impossible to see through the waterdrops which veiled me – too heavy to sweep away with the hand – but I could hear Fitz yelp as the hard-driven rain whipped into her. Within the wail of the wind and the lash of the wet there was a sea-noise – the light burbling roar it makes as it runs quickly across the flat easy sand. The rain passed over us – moving darkly along the coast towards Saltstreet quay – I could see out again. Close, the waves came towards us – each overlapping the last – outdistancing themselves as they ran ever forward.

Hesketh was still standing – her hair weighted down with its burden of water – her long coat hanging heavy about her, blowing only slowly in the fierce wind. She looked like the statue of some deity alighting from flight – draperies streaming in the force of her descent – but frozen into stone. I could hear her exhortation to the whale – 'Come, my friend, hold out, only a short time now' – run on like the sea's incantatory water-sound. Yet she looked exhausted. Fitz stood beside her – hair all straightened and darkened into a smooth bathing cap – clothes sculpted into a waterfall. I thought of walking with her across miles of sand through the light-netted water – ankle-deep and still – so utterly unlike the racing waves whipped up and driven in by the wind.

Fitz gestured with her doused rifle at Crambo standing on the dunes with two of the soldiers – too distant to see which of them – or what they intended. I was looking that way when the first wave struck my legs, pouring seawater into my boots. As though it had met a rock lying half-submerged in sand – the water divided to surge up the whale's flanks on either side – splashing spray up onto her dark back. Hesketh staggered as Fitz ran to her side – we linked arms together – like a row of dancers standing ready to sway back or leap forward. The water was almost too deep and swift-running to keep our footing in – so we were driven back – but the whale still lay only semi-submerged – flailing a little before collapsing again.

'It's going to get swept further in,' Fitz shouted. 'It isn't trying.'

'Go on,' Hesketh called in her ringing voice. 'Go, dear creature.'

And we joined in – waving our arms – calling out to the whale – 'Hurry now, take your chance, go on.' I heard Crambo's cries mingling with the rest – his odd slurred bark – then Stevens' mild curt voice. The soldiers – all three of them – were in the water with us – urging the whale away from the dangerous shore. We retreated – holding on to each other to keep upright – still urgently calling on our whale to swim away.

'Is it dead?' Fitz cried – but nobody answered.

Then – just in the way the tide sometimes lifts the lazing seals from their sandbanks and floats them unwillingly off – we saw the island of whaleback rise buoyantly – move. The whale stirred – released back into her own element again – and quickly – so suddenly we were unprepared to see it –

178

whisked herself about – was off. For a brief while we could trace a dark curve rising sometimes in the wave-valleys – or the spray-burst as her head broke the surface – but then she must have dived. She was gone.

Fitz

We laughed, capered on the beach, shook hands, hugged and clapped each other on the back. Fierce sun engulfed us from a fissure in bright purple cloud. Unaware of our painfully cold bodies, trembling knees, lost voices, waterlogged skin, chattering teeth, we gambolled there like shipwrecked mariners cast up on solid ground. Every few moments someone would look out through the telescope, but we had no sighting of the whale. It never came back. There are stories of the creatures returning again to their rescuers, too disoriented or damaged to escape their end on land, but others are restored to wellbeing once they are free. This one, we must presume, went on its way.

'Hesketh,' I said, 'this tide must be up two hours early, at least.'

She smiled.

'Severe weather warning tonight, I'm afraid,' Stevens said apologetically, as though his fault. 'I expect the marsh will be covered again.'

Crambo nodded vehemently at this, but he wouldn't come in to get warm even though Hesketh, to my amazement, asked him. He went off back to his lair, but apparently on good terms with the soldiers – of whom Kezia remarked rather tartly that they had appeared at just the right moment, *after* we'd carried the water. At least, I said, at least... It could have been a bad moment, but it became a curiously good one. There was that instant when we all stood in the sea, our joint effort directed into a useless pacific act, a common bond. I told her about the time I was driving late at night, rather fast perhaps, along the side of Hampstead Heath, when the headlights showed a fox's cautious, elegant dog-face as it stepped out to cross the road. There was no time to brake, cars behind would catch it if I swerved. In desperation I sounded the horn in warning so that the fox glanced up, saw me, darted back from the sound as though I had been able to speak, tell it not to step out, not now.

We were up late last night with hot baths, hot toddys, talking late in front of the fire wrapped in rugs. The tide filled the marsh to the brim again so that the boathouse felt like the Ark, grounded on an uncomfortably low hill, but the water subsided at its due time. In the morning the car was able to drive across the wet causeway splashing just enough to cause a rainbow-arc of water-drops. There is a touch of coolness now, even in the sun, the dipping down toward autumn. Before I left I went down to the beach on my own, before the others were up. It was the first time I've seen the dawn at Saltstreet; the first time, I thought with amusement, that I'd been so avid for the day. The sea was still, stiller than I have ever seen it, hardly a ripple stirring. On the horizon there was a rose-gold line of light, so narrow it might have been sliced by a bird's flight, yet bright enough to tint the whole darkness into deep grey, pale silver, triumphant white. The beauty of it was so quiet, so absolute, it seemed like a gift from the sea to the watcher. If Aphrodite had risen out of the waves on her scallop shell, the vision would have seemed merely appropriate. As the opening sun fired the grey sea brighter each moment, I confronted that great mass of water, let myself apprehend its completeness for the first time. In some sense unknown to me before it spoke of peace.

On my way back up to the house I came suddenly face-to-face with Crambo. I know better now than to try to speak to him, but to my surprise he came out with a long peroration, perhaps about the whale. Taking it as a farewell speech, I offered him my penknife – a parting gift I thought he might find

181

useful. After considering it closely on my outstretched hand, not without a tinge of suspicion perhaps, he snatched it, ran away a short distance, examined it, turned to give me a dazzling smile. It was, I feel, our most successful communication.

When I said goodbye to Hesketh, still unmade-up in her royal kimono, I felt a curious tic of doubt, a silenced alarm-bell, that I will ever see her again. We shook hands, then she embraced me warmly in a miasma of scent and whisky. It was an effort not to shed ill-omened tears. She appeared to me then as I hope I always treated her: like some great lady of the stage brought low by time to the corner of the bar, but still able on occasion to lift her head, speak some speech as no one else yet can. To Kezia, pale as an owl, I said, as though someone else had scripted the words, 'I'll come back.' She did not reply. I put my much-increased luggage in the car, drove off across the marsh, waving until they were out of sight behind the tall grasses.

It wasn't the driver I knew, but she was friendly enough, a Scot, asked if my billet had been decent. I told her it had; good people. She said I was lucky, she'd heard a few stories... By lunchtime I was on the train to London, my hands still salt-soaked from caressing the whale. I have Meredith's last letter in my pocket, a talisman, my touchstone while I cannot touch her. Apart from the practical proposals for meeting me at the station, she continues our conversations about life, work, the two combined inextricably into homecoming. I sigh, put the letter back in my inside pocket, against my heart. I know the end verbatim already, it says:

I would follow you, as you know, to the end of the world, but I am so happy that you are coming back to me in London instead – not only so much more convenient but, to me, very romantic. I will welcome you back as best I can.

Crambo

I saw him go, her go, Trousers, the one Kezia liked best, off
he went with all his bags and his rucksack, all the things they
gave him, and the car whizzed along the road so fast that
where its shadow fell on the wall of rushes it flickered like
firelight. If I'd been a dog I'd have thrown myself barking to
bite at the wheels, and so what if it killed me. The noise of
the sea was inside my head that day, like when you put your
ears under water and it throbs in there, booming. Stevens
came looking for me, wandering round in the dunes calling
Crambo, but I didn't answer, I didn't want to know.

 I think about the whale, not a fish, a whale, swimming out
there maybe somewhere deep where the water goes black far
down dark as eyes shut, maybe asleep, floating and rolling
like a coloured glass bottle juggled on the sea's lap, maybe
jumping high across the wave-dips, crest to crest, laughing
when he landed. I wished I was sitting on his back, riding
him, like Hesketh can. But She let him go.

There is death on the beach at each tide, crabs turned turtle
with their once crook'd claws limply open, silver fish draped
in seaweed-loops like rain fragments on a gorse bush, whelk
shells drilled through to the naked whorls inside, birds in
twists of shattered feathers. The sea takes their breath away,
exchanges it for death, everyone knows this is fair. All of the
things the sea changes, life returns, hermits in empty shells,
barnacles growing on crabs, shell to sand, sand to worm,
worm to fish, fish to Crambo, and back again, Crambo picked
clean by sea-creatures, Crambo-bone ground down by the
pebbles into sand, and round again, *breath, death, death,*
breath. I am the beach.

Meredith

Something wonderful has happened here. Oh, the joy! The lights are back on – to welcome you, Fitz, to rejoice over your dear recovered ma. At least, they're restored dimly, to a moonlight level, only in some places with caution, but no more that utter blackness throughout as though the world had abruptly ended. London is en fête, the more so for the contrast between the places where it's happening and the black holes where it's not. Some haven't dared to remove their blackout curtains yet; others, more bold, put candles in their windows as though it's some feast day. The low light is delightful, a fairyland of sparkle like a Christmas pantomime scene or the most charming party. People wander about the streets marvelling. Even the rain looks beautiful, with the lights reflecting in the wet pavements, the lamps circled with drops of brightness. There's something tender about it, poignant; the softness like nursery nightlights gently illuminating a city. Soon the brightness will be back, but this temporary in-between state has its delights too. It is indescribably romantic.

Lights in the dusk have always moved me, I don't know why. It reminds me of looking out from my room into the garden late at night, long ago, after my parents had gone to bed, when the lights of all the other windows showed through the trees. All the houses had those old tall windows looking out over the gardens at the back, showing their lights companionably after dark, keeping them on late while the sound of people laughing, talking, sitting out, drifted quietly up to me.

Here, the balcony is hardly more than a narrow wrought iron ledge really, in front of windows down to the floor, so one sits almost still half within the room with knees outside, in a rather silly way which is charming when it's hot (and not inconvenient when it rains suddenly). I like the sensation that all around other people, one's invisible neighbours, are enjoying the same thing, out in their yards or perched on the window ledges, with just the clink of a glass or a murmur to indicate their presences. This summer it will be low-lit out there, a Victorian scene; next summer, if all goes well, the lights will blaze. I like to think of us lounging here, windows open, with a candle in a bottle answering the starlight.

Kezia

After Fitz had gone, I went with Hesketh to the studio – we drank coffee and watched the weather out of her picture windows – the clouds still whirling round the sky – dementedly departing and returning. *I'll come back*. Fitz had finished all her jobs before she left – there was nothing to be done. The portrait of me stood unfinished on the easel – I could not contemplate sitting for it now – there seemed no point – Hesketh did not suggest it. Perhaps we knew it would never be finished.

'Do you realise, Kezia,' Hesketh said, 'the war is almost over?'

'Fitz said so. She said we've won.'

We surveyed the ruined beach in silence for a moment.

'When she was hurt, that was the last wave of bombing, or so it seems. It's the end of it now. So you mustn't worry too much about her in London. This will be finished soon, even in Europe.'

'But they still mined our beach?'

'That is another question. Just a muddle, d'you think? In case of some mad counter-invasion was probably the theory. We could ask Corporal Stevens, but I doubt he would really know. All of the things that have been done in order to win, nobody will explain, especially now. Who is accountable? Were they justified? How will we ever forgive each other? Fighting evil is a dirty business, isn't it?'

'Fitz told me...' – my most frequent phrase – '...that everyone keeps saying nothing will ever be the same again.'

Hesketh gazed outwards, unblinking.

'Nothing is ever the same,' she said at length. 'We know that. Sometimes it's a great relief that it isn't. So, shall we move on, when we can?'

'What about your work?'

'Perhaps I'll do other work, if we go somewhere else. Perhaps I'll have to sacrifice it – for a while.'

When Hesketh said this, I was afraid. Her work had been a sort of permanence for me – a wherefore – a constant. I could not imagine anywhere else – I had only faint memories of another studio with other, brighter paintings. But Hesketh talked on about places we might go – work I might do – until I half-believed that she meant it, for the moment. I didn't say that my only work had lain in enabling hers – I had no talents or qualifications for any other job – she spoke of colleges and training schools as though such places might be possible for me. In her words was the implication that we had endured here for so long – after our shipwreck – but now the place wasn't the same any more – they had finally taken it from us by making it not as it had been – impossible for us to stay. I didn't say that I only wanted Fitz to come back here to us – not for us to follow her into some unknown brave new world. I just agreed, as I used to when Hesketh talked about things I didn't really understand.

She said, with her rapturous smile, 'It's your birthright.'

'The city?'

'To have everything.'

Fitz

London is as Meredith said. Meredith is as she promised in her letters. Everything is as I hoped; delight persists. The prospect of happiness opens out before me like a sudden view come upon by chance over the brow of a tree-crowned hill, the city with all its possibilities lit up below, the river widening through it to the sea, the downs rising grey-green on the other side, beauty reaching far into the distance. Already, as she said we would, we've walked in the streets in the evening to look at the lights with the other people in the summer's-end crowd, lain on the grass in the park with our picnic, queued for theatre seats in the gods, eaten late in obscure restaurants, kept long nights awake. Then at the weekend we never went out but turned the time around, only getting up at dusk to sit at her balcony window in a dream. Even these few days have seemed like a full season of life. On the mornings she has to go to work I walk with her, spend the day wandering round museums, galleries, bookshops, wait to meet her afterwards. One afternoon when it rained I went to the cinema. I sent Hesketh and Kezia a postcard of Piccadilly Circus, with all its tawdry lights on.

Yesterday was one of those days which enforced a brief absence. After having my lunch in a cheap café full of dazed scholars who'd come out of the Museum reading room for a rare brush with the daylight, I went to look at the house. I took a bus along Camden, up Haverstock Hill, then walked across the corner of the Heath – the familiar route. As I walked beside the ponds I saw the kingfisher – not the blue lightning flashing from tree to tree, but a slow glide over the bright water, the full length of the pool, in a long coruscating banner of welcome. Down the hill on the other side, under the railway bridge, there was the cobbled alley as it always had been, enfolded in its inexplicable quiet. The house looked, as Meredith had said, as if it were in hibernation. I walked round the curved corner of the garden wall, tried the gate, but the lock was firmly rusted. Over the brick top of the wall I could see the small apple tree already bowed with its load of fruit, the unpruned white rose still flourishing, its scent drifting down the alley.

I remembered very vividly my mother sitting outside the back door on days like this, reading, with her deckchair set to catch the sun, the uncut grass pillowing round her scattered with petals. It was so strong a vision, I felt that if I climbed up to look over the wall I'd see her there as she always had been, entire in herself, present. It seemed impossible that I could envisage her so clearly unless she was indeed just on the other side of the wall, reading in the garden. There was an acute sense of certainty, of absolute restoration to an original state of rightness, which contained me, my hand on the door latch, the garden, everything. For a few heartbeats time's divisions shimmered, dissolved; the things-that-had-been embraced the things-yet-to-come, seamlessly. Then the noisy slow drumroll of a train echoed down from the bridge; I stirred, reached to pick some of the roses which were nodding down to me as a gift for Meredith.

As I took my flowers I heard a faint sound from inside the garden, perhaps a stifled laugh. I scrambled up on top of a dustbin to look over the wall, balanced on it insecurely to gaze down at the uncut grass scattered with petals, the woman seated on a deckchair set just outside the back door to catch the sun. She was reading. As I clutched onto the wall top like some cartoon burglar she looked up; her face was transformed as mine must have been, she cried, 'Fitz, oh, my dear. You got my telegram! You're here!' Then, more practically, 'But darling, why not come round to the door?'

The lid of the bin crashed to the ground as I jumped down, ran to the front door, which was unlocked, rushed through the house in fear that she might have vanished when I burst out into the garden. But she was still there, holding out her arms.

'When I saw the house like this,' she said, 'I thought you might be gone too ...'

Kezia

The weather was wild – unsettled – all that week – the tide stayed high as it sometimes did in autumn when an onshore wind would not let it ebb away – so that each inflow rose higher on the back of the one before. I asked Hesketh to read aloud after supper – as she had when I was a child – her voice easily outreaching the elements outside. As she did, I listened with all my power – but at the same time I had an inward picture of our future here – islanded – without any prospect. It had never struck me so forcibly before that – although I was young and Hesketh not yet old – we had finite time left. She would die one day surrounded by her work – lie in state among her pictures like a dragon with its hoard – while I had nothing to show for my existence – except myself. I thought grimly that before Fitz came here, with her other certainties, I had never been discontent. Now, for the first time, I knew what was meant by a dilemma – unwilling to go yet not certain of staying.

One windy afternoon a young man came to the door – at first I didn't recognise him in his leather jacket and corduroys – a humanised Stevens.

'So sorry to intrude,' he said – talking to Hesketh rather than to me. 'I thought you'd be pleased to know that we're leaving now.'

'All of you?'

He nodded. 'You don't require our protection any more, if you ever did.'

To end the silence which followed, I made myself thank him for helping us with the whale.

'I'll never forget that,' he said. 'Thank you both for that. I'd have given anything to see a whale like that, and there it was. I know it's spoiled your privacy, having us on the beach all the time, so you'll have it to yourselves again now – you and Crambo. But it's been wonderful for me.'

We all shook hands with a kind of last-minute cordiality – slightly spoiled by his exhortation to be careful of the mines – a reminder that they would leave their litter behind them. I resisted telling him that Crambo would deal with his shore. Hesketh wished him well, wherever they were going – Italy? Greece? – raised her eyebrows at me in caricature amazement as the door closed on him.

'Who'd have thought?' she said mischievously. 'Aren't they charming when they go?'

That night the storm continued. The wind seemed to whirl the sea impatiently up into a fabric roll of blue-black silk – throw the whole bolt forward to land unravelling at our feet. High tide arrived suddenly – deep outside the back door – covering the dry foreshore sand – the lower dunes – the mined beach – rushing up the inlets and creeks to overflow the marsh. Our range of higher dunes stuck up above it – a wavering wall of camel-hump watchtowers – we could see the straight bank top of the seawall beside the overflowing ditch running inland alongside the marsh – it was still dry. But the house shook – reverberated – with each wave that thudded against its low bank of shingle – I felt the slow backflow of the undertow tugging at the foundations. In the morning the water had only receded a little – the same strong wind was pushing the rumpled fabric close against the foreshore.

'This is like a spring tide,' Hesketh said. 'Do you think we should get out the canoe?'

The canoe was one of our jokes – it was in the shed – enormously heavy, elaborately carved, Hiawatha-stylised – ordered perhaps from some Edwardian catalogue but never used – too heavy for anyone to carry as far as the sea.

'Perhaps later,' I replied ritualistically. 'We might even be able to float it out.'

Indeed, the next high tide came over the yard-island – up to the front doorstep of the house. The waves were smaller (I thought) – there were still some lone islands of dune-peaks – and the top of the ditch-bank like a straight Roman bridge.

'Do you think Crambo has gone inland?'

'I'm sure. He'll be up by his mother's house. A good thing the soldiers have gone, too. Their hole must be flooded out.'

Fastidious, I refused to speculate on their damp fate.

We agreed that – in the morning – if the storm looked set to continue for a third day – we would cross the causeway while we could – when the tide was at its lowest – go inland.

'An adventure,' said Hesketh.

Crambo

Usually when the water comes up high, overflows the marsh like sea soup boiling over, one of my places stays dry. There's a place out of the wind, a low hollow in the dunes where the stinging sand lies still even when the beach air is all thick with gnats of sand-grains, another place that's a cool place, down at the marsh edge where I can lie in deep shade on a green pad of damp flattened grass and pant like a hot dog. When it's bitter cold, there's a place where I light a fire in a great tin drum, down in the dip between four hillocks like the hole in a big tooth, and I made a shelter there, a roof across the top with open holes landward and seaward. It's mostly cold. But there was a dry place too, along towards the wishbone, where the dunes turn into a little gravelly cliff with its shells and stones all arranged in neat stripes, layers licked by the sea's tongue. Up on the top there was a prong, a pinnacle with a big stone balancing on it, which always stayed dry. I've been stuck sitting up there, rocking on the stone, singing to myself, for hours at a time, waiting for the sea to turn round and give me back my island. But only that one time it floated me off, like a seal swirled off the sandbank by the fierce running tide.

The waves were different, each one long from its first curve far out to the final breaking, overhanging forever before the plunge into spray. They covered the wreck, even the mast top, and came on, up the beach and over the dunes to meet the overflowing marsh water. All the sandbags and barbed wire were tossed about like floats and streamers. I laughed and hugged myself and danced on my big stone, until I saw what else was happening. Then I thought about my mother, locked inside that cave with the waves pounding on the door as though she could answer, and then bursting in and rushing up the stairs, going in to her room. I knew I would have to go inside as well, and get her before the sea could steal her forever.

Fitz

Meredith woke me. We were in her bed, in her beautiful untidy bedroom, with clothes on the floor, flowers on the windowsill, a view of chimney pots and tree crowns. It smelt of treacle, quince, distant coffee. My watch had stopped. I stirred when Meredith brushed the hair back from my forehead; as she leant forward her silk stained-glass-coloured dressing gown opened to show her body like the light within.

'Fitz,' she said, in the particular way she has of saying it. 'Mac just phoned.' (Mac has a wireless, is a source of news.) 'There's been a great flood up on the coast, near Saltstreet. The sea has gone a long way inland, they've evacuated a lot of people.'

'Has anyone been drowned?'

'She doesn't know; I did ask. The navy and the coastguard are rescuing people off rooftops. The news is about that, nothing about any casualties.'

The shifting sun-outlined shadows of the leaves printed her trees on the wall behind the bed.

'I'll have to go.'

'Yes, I know. Shall I come with you?'

'Do you think we can get there?'

'We can try.'

When I heard Meredith say 'we', even in the midst of my fear I was overcome with delight. The pain of my anxiety for Hesketh and Kezia was confused with the pain of leaving Meredith's bed (both love-induced hurts, but different in kind). In the end, I had to go alone; it wasn't possible for us both to get tickets, travel passes, all the paraphernalia of emergency zones. As it was, we told many lies to evidence the true fact that I had to go; only my boss's intervention was finally effective. I was armed with all this, all Meredith's provisions and exhortations. She never tried to prevent me from returning to Saltstreet, never tried to conceal her dislike of it. My mother was the same; it was hard to miss seeing her again that day too, though she told me we would soon get used to the idea that we could meet any time.

It was nearly evening before I started on the strange boat-journey across the fields. Trees wading up to their waists in rippling water is a familiar sight, in flooded water meadows down by their rivers, where the willows welcome such inundations. But I had never seen before, except in dim photographs, houses armpit-deep straining to stand firm against the waterflow. It was a dreamlike floating, down little streets where the roofs were near, as though the buildings were just one-storeyed, but doorless, low-browed over the new canal. Everything was very quiet. I thought of the people from these houses, selling dressed crab out of their sitting room windows downstairs, taking chairs out onto sunny doorsteps, living inland, waking one night to find the sea running up the street. They mostly had boats, though, or the people next door did; they were gone.

My boat was borrowed from some of those fishing neighbours, exhausted now, who'd been out all day salvaging what they could of people's ruined possessions, rescuing the left-behind, the animals, forgotten treasures. It had been hard to convince them that there was anyone at the boathouse, but once they remembered that there was talk about someone living there, they were willing enough. I asked if they knew what had happened to the soldiers; they told me that all the machine-gun crews on shore defences had just left, so they were no help to the naval rescue, but at least didn't need saving. The coastguard, the lifeboats, the fishing fleet that

197

had gone to Dunkirk, had all been out since dawn, working this alien seascape. The vessel I was lent was one of those tiny open fishing boats, a glorified rowing-dinghy, with nothing but an upright doorless cupboard set to shelter the wheel, no cabin. It had got back from Dunkirk, so they reckoned it would take me across the marsh.

In the dreamlike silence I navigated along these unfamiliar waterways, following the line where the creek had been – although it surely would have been possible to take a shorter route floating high above the marsh. Far over to the left, westwards, I recognised the church tower rising out of the sea itself like a revenant from one of the fabled drowned villages. How many miles inland must the water reach? An aeroplane came over, quite low, slow, perhaps searching for those imagined survivors stranded in treetops or drifting on the eddies which twirled their barn-door rafts. I passed strange things floating randomly by, great unidentifiable tangles like giant hair-combings, odd planks with buttressed wooden blocks in unexpected colours with bright patches and inexplicable numbers. Once there was a boat's hull just below water level, a sheeted ghost nosing along half-invisible. Seabirds gave the boat the comic askance looks which they also accorded the flotsam which bobbed with them on the waves.

It was a sinister dream. The boat moved slowly, the sun was hidden by an ochre-tinged solid sky. It was so hard to see any distance clearly that I felt a momentary panic in case my eyesight was failing; terror overtaking my previous unease about losing my way, running out of fuel. There was no sign of the boathouse, which surely should have been in sight now, aligned between the church tower and the obscure horizon. But the boatman had said, 'There's a lot of water about.

Could well be over the roof by now.' Meredith had made me promise not to do anything dangerous, out in the dark or the storm; we had not imagined this slower quest. It was like some inundation at the end of the world, everything dissolving into nothingness, covered with great waters. As the light failed I moved slowly back and forth, searching, straining to understand what floated on the water, to peer down through its muddy veil interpreting what still stood beneath. It was cold.

Meredith

We have a pact not to imagine misfortune, among our other alliances, so I do not think of anything but good homecoming – the strong spell which worked so well before. But perhaps it would compliment you to know, Fitz, you with your lonely pride, self-sufficiency, hunger, that I slept badly without you, already so used to your warm presence beside me, missed you, thought of you constantly through the long evening. I telephoned Mac to hear about the weather forecast: bad with worse to come. There is an undeniable romance, in the literary sense, to lying alone in bed while one's lover rides a rough sea, lovely on the water, but as an actual experience I could well do without it, even so. I comforted myself with the thought of Kezia's caul. Western wind, when wilt thou blow, that the small rain down shall rain…

Today, early, I rang the long-suffering Mac again: still high water on the leaky houseboat. No news otherwise, so we must presume no more incursions of that wild sea, the tempest abated. After work I went to buy some theatre tickets for next week – a good omen. On the way home, I came down the steps beside Somerset House to the river. It was still sunny on that side, there were people dawdling over the bridge, leaning on the embankment balustrades, looking up at St Paul's, the dome so heartrendingly visible at the moment, soaring resplendent above everything with magnificent irony. I went to look over the wall at the river as well, the water was high, a tug boat was setting out with washing still fluttering from the funnel like bunting, the sailors waving at the departing shore. The water was not exactly clear, even with poetic licence, but it looked bright, the light was buoyant on it, the colours were pure.

I don't exactly know whether I prayed for you or to you, Fitz; it's a long time since I prayed in any of the usual senses, but standing there in the sun I did ask whatever powers there may be to keep you safe while you're gone from me. That cold stone struck through to my flesh, chill, with the dull indifference of the world to all the lovers who are parted; I heard the laments of us all. (Christ, that my love were in my arms, and I in my bed again.) *The river answered, or perhaps the sea itself, moving into her arms with a shudder of joy; we are together still, we are not separated, everything is here. I thought of your dawn seascape, the sense of transfiguration, infinite solace, acceptance, which flowed over you then, not to be wrested from the waters by determination or supplication, but suddenly casually bestowed. But Fitz, you had your vigil at Saltstreet to purify you, heal you, prepare you for that moment. I'm not a questing knight, but a very tired woman, waiting to hear individual news in this life, hoping the river's mercy is for me now, that love will prevail this time.*

Kezia

In the morning, the causeway was impassable – I realised the tide wasn't going to ebb enough for us to get back to the mainland – on the marsh, the water would remain. All the waterways were sunk – merged into one pathless wetland. The Rayburn's fire had gone out – quenched by the sea which had inched under the door and now surprisingly eddied and swirled about the kitchen floor. Hesketh wore her wellington boots with her kimono to pack a box of kitchen supplies for upstairs. She made coffee on the stove in the studio – set up a makeshift camp there. I rescued some books, our coats, my logbook – as I carried it upstairs it reminded me – like a childhood friend (almost like Crambo) – that the high tide was still to come. This was the lull.

Already the yard was invisible underwater – our horseshoe of buildings seemed to float on a wind-flecked mere extending far inland. When I slid out of the kitchen window the lake was not too deep to paddle in, but its tide tugged at my legs. I waded over to the shed – its door pinned open by the current – and peered into the darkness. The familiar junk inside was floating – jostling – bumping against the walls – spinning frivolously. Even the earthbound canoe had lifted from its usual slant. I towed it out – with the strange semblance of leading a horse from the stable – tethered it on a long rope.

Hesketh had dressed – gathered together a nest of blankets – an archaic pile of lanterns and candle ends – her favourite astrakhan overcoat.

'I've got Hiawatha out. It's floating.'

'Oh, surely it won't come to that – the water won't come so high?'

'It might. We can get out onto the roof.'

'*My paintings.*'

I thought – she won't leave her studio – it's like the captain on the bridge – she can't abandon her ship. And if it would be death to her to go – she might as well stay.

'Hesketh, we might have to. We can take them with us – some of them. If it comes to that, the lifeboat will come for us. We'll have to be ready.'

'And where are those precious soldiers when we need them? I thought their entire function was to guard us, to rescue us, or at least you, Kezia. At the first sign of trouble, they've vanished.'

While the water rose, we drank coffee – played bezique – laced the coffee with rum. Occasionally I glanced at the sea level – with seafarer's detachment, I hoped. Sometimes we felt the foundations shift beneath us – the tremor as the house clung to them. Hesketh said once – 'I'm sorry, Kezia, I can't send it back. It's still part of calling it up before, I think, I don't know. Maybe. But I can't do anything now. I have tried. No go Blavatsky.'

In the afternoon we began to pack up her paintings – the smaller wood panels into an old canvas bag – some of the larger ones into a makeshift portfolio. There was a tea-chest too, in case anybody came for us in something bigger than the canoe. To see Hesketh choose – try to decide – move about among her work touching some things and ignoring others – was like witnessing a person abandon their memory of life thus far. For her, it must have been a kind of death. Yet she was as dignified – as fatalistic – as if she'd always known it would come to this – the sacrificial loss into the deep water – not the flame.

When the sea was high under the upstairs windows I retrieved the canoe – with difficulty – hauled it in close –

discarded the tether which had become the anchor-rope –
awkwardly wriggled into it from the sill. It was gracious and
stable – heavy as I paddled it round the house – with room
on board for a whole house party of weekend guests. I tied
it up to the latch of the studio window where it rocked like
a miniature Viking longship in an unlikely fjord. Hesketh
passed me out the bags – the portfolio like a hoisted sail – the
blankets and foodboxes – Hiawatha swallowed them all. The
house moved perceptibly – with a grinding noise like some
vast industrial process – some mining or blasting or earth-
moving – to which people should not be too close.

'Hesketh, we must go.'

She stood there in the middle of the studio with her coat
flying about her in the gale from the open window and wailed
– formally – in a cry like a ritualistic mourning-howl at a
wake – a keening litany not of despair but of plain sorrow.
It seemed inhuman to stop her – but I wanted her to stop.
Another wave struck the house so that it reverberated dully
– a broken bell – suddenly she was practical – unafraid –
even humorous. Calmly, we manoeuvred ourselves into place
in our ark – laughed about our inexpert rowing – set off
cautiously landwards.

As we made our way – laboriously – over-loaded – we saw
an extraordinary sight. Towards us, across the marsh-mere,
came a vessel even more strange than the canoe – a high raft
constructed of oil-drums and tomato-tins, fishing net floats
and discarded life buoys – topped with a five-barred gate, an
old mattress, a pile of eiderdowns and cushions. Lying curled
up on these – like a spiral sea shell or an ancient ammonite
– was an unmoving old woman – set by her rheumatism
into this whirligig mould. In the water – swimming with
the repellent efficiency of a rat – was Crambo – in harness –

towing the craft along behind him – the rudder rope in his teeth. It was almost frightening to see the determination in his face – the strength with which he propelled his makeshift vessel against the tide to be the salvation of those otherwise forgotten. I waved – called out his name.

'Crambo, at any rate, has come to your rescue,' Hesketh observed. 'Disappointing for him that we'd done it already, but most characteristic of you.'

He swam on to join us – a carthorse turned amphibian – with his precious cargo towering ungainly behind him – his face transformed with relief – almost beautiful.

Fitz

When I knew I was not going to find the boathouse, or even discover where it had been, I stopped ploughing up and down, there and back; the boat drifted, almost still. I lit the two small lamps, although it was only dusk; a few stars, in reflection, showed between the drizzly clouds. There was still some tea left in the flask Meredith had given me, so I drank some. (She and I had shared the flask lid for our cup, once, far away.) The idea of her there sustained me. It was too cold to cry, or even think much. I did realise that perhaps Hesketh and Kezia were among the rescued. It wasn't impossible that they had been taken somewhere else, to another village hall, or some big house, or an inland hospital. But no one knew of them. There was no news of Crambo, either. I'd seen nothing floating which could be a body, except a drowned sheep's carcase spinning stately in its private whirlpool.

Cautiously I took the little boat shorewards, not up the memory map of the channel, but across where the sea wall had stood, up towards the church. I reckoned there was plenty of depth for this small vessel, but chugged along dead slow. It seemed only decent to try to see what had happened to Crambo, to his ma in her cottage, in the limited time left before I had to turn back. I almost gave up: the church tower seemed to retreat before me; it would have taken half the time to stroll along the causeway to the church green. Just as I was beginning to despair of ever reaching it, there appeared a light flickering ahead, insubstantial yet beckoning as summer campfires on old-fashioned holidays, before blackouts and war-darkness.

As the boat moved – so gradually – closer, I discerned something like a magic carpet riding above the water, a floor of spread light, modestly lit up like a little stage at a country fair or a square in some foreign town. It hovered in the darkness, the only thing that was bright anywhere, inexplicable. It was not the deck of a boat: too square, too low in the water, with no rigging or railing. I heard singing and laughter come clear across the water from that isle of the blessed. I looked, gazed, could not understand what I saw.

When I came near, the lighted floor resolved itself into the flat roof of the church porch, its platform still protruding a few feet above the water, like a square rock with the cliff of the bell tower, the sloping foothills of the main roof, rising into darkness around it. There was a fire burning in an oil-drum brazier, candles and lamps ranged about the low parapet at the edge, creating an incongruous impression of party. Moored against this mirage were strange ships, a huge ramshackle raft like a Dark-Age chariot, a miniscule dragon-prowed longship with a solid sail. Approaching at last, I could recognise the ones I was seeking: Hesketh, Kezia, Crambo, an ancient lady bent into an arc. They were talking, drinking, cooking on their storytellers' stove, as though high water had not driven them there, as though there was nowhere in the world they would rather be, no other company to be preferred. When I called out to them they waved hospitably, not with the desperation of the saved.

Only Kezia ran to the edge of her tower, crying my name, adding, 'You've come back!' as though I'd dropped in for supper while on holiday, rather than waded through hell and high water – perforce leaving my love behind – in order to find them. They welcomed me onto their life-raft with the same offhand largesse they'd shown when I arrived lost on their doorstep, before this strange summer. I had to moor my boat, clamber onto the roof, warm my hands at the fire; to refuse would have seemed churlish. I felt, far from intrepid, slightly ridiculous, as though I'd made rather a fuss about nothing.

It was almost difficult to persuade my friends to leave their lucky refuge, while the faintest tinge of daylight lasted, return with me to the dull world of blankets, hot water bottles, strong tea, disinfectant baths, and the telephone. On the slow journey back, trailing our outlandish small craft, there was a distinct sense of returning from an outing. We finished Hesketh's brandy, Crambo crooned to himself, Kezia held my arm tightly.

'We were just paddling shorewards in our flotilla with Crambo,' Hesketh said to me, 'when the boathouse disappeared. It was there, grumbling somewhat but standing fast, then it vanished, completely as a sand-castle dissolving into the water.'

'Gone, gone,' Crambo agreed.

'Not the studio, Hesketh?' I said. 'All your work.'

Hesketh swept the collar of her astrakhan coat up higher, an elegant, broken gesture.

'Ah, well,' she said, lightly. 'This rough magic...'

Now they all sleep, these dispossessed ones; that longest of days has ended. I can go home tomorrow; perhaps they will come with me after all. This inland refuge cannot keep them long. As I lie here in this hotel bed – without my love, too tired to rest – I try to remember Saltstreet, how it was when I arrived, lost. But I have half-forgotten that strange place; it vanishes as surely as the old islands that sink back into the sea though their bells never cease to sound. As though summoned by imagination, only maintained by a will which has faltered, nothing now remains of it but a dream, a haunting. It seems one of those sea-pictures, a trick of the elements, light dancing on the waves in the semblance of island or harbour, a vision whipped up by the wind, projected on clouds. And then the storm recedes, to leave only a wild joy.

Meredith

Letters written at night, in bed, to people who will be seen the next day, are the preserve of lovers – perhaps unhappy ones who must hand each other the furtive diaries of their separation. But happy as we are, Fitz, I must continue our cut-short conversation (as I will always) to tell you – while it is still with me, before it's forgotten in the pleasure of being together – that when I heard your voice on the telephone just now, all was well with me again. The dark was overwhelmed.

Though you sounded tired, your voice was like a benediction to me, of healing, of comfort (though I should add in the interests of veracity that I could hear you cursing in the most unholy manner as you rattled through your pockets for more change). Only you would announce your epic rescue of the abandoned, half-drowned, sea-ravaged, with an anecdote about finding the hotel – though I am sorry the dinner was so bad. Only you would know that, however late, I would be waiting for news of you. Never anything more welcome than that. Sweet rain.

The river – whoever – the powers we pray to in adversity – did not mock my anxiety, but recognised my love. When I think for how long you held at bay thoughts of horror, to be rewarded at last by the restoration, I honour you again; it was only a brief while I had to keep the faith, but it was hard. My imagination is too powerful to be easily drugged, but now I am a little ashamed of my fears, though I did not let them conquer, for as you know I believe in the triumph of love.

When I heard you like that – however distant, however stilted – I knew that the world was safe on its course, its weathers calm, its trees sheltering late travellers, its waters still. I knew that the stars were guiding the seafarers home, that the moon tempers the city's darkness, that we will sleep in safety. Then morning.

Kezia

When I saw Fitz – looking like the ferryman come to fetch us – in that battered old boat with the little lamps glittering like Christmas tree candles – I suddenly understood how I loved her. My prince had come – I realised – but I didn't recognise him – or not soon enough. My emotions – so tidal – so extreme – had not resolved themselves for me into the state – love – so well known to me from books, music, art. It had swept over me – unnamed, invisible – a freak wave which retreated, leaving me breathless but unmoved. I was so anxious not to be a princess that I refused my chance to be rescued – if that moment was not illusory too. Hesketh tried to give me my freedom – in the only way she knew how – but I didn't take it. Now Fitz had come back – so soon, so suddenly – there would be much rejoicing that we had found each other again – found ourselves – escaped the great storm to begin anew. But I knew she hadn't come back for me – but to fulfil an obligation – I had lost her.

I knew that certainly as I witnessed her behaviour then – her tact with Hesketh – her politeness to Crambo's poor ma – her quiet collusion with me about helping them. She stopped Crambo being taken inside – let him return to the church green on his raft to await the waters' receding – even deflected the canteen volunteers' disapproval when he took the sandwich they proffered – licked the fish-paste from its interstices – threw the mystifying bread slices away. Her authority saved us many indignities – I realised how dependable she was – she would visit Crambo's ma in the cottage hospital – she would drive us to a nice hotel – she would never let us down. It was only right that she should also take trouble to telephone.

I still have the picture – Hesketh's portrait of Fitz – her ordeal on the beach – it was one of the ones which was saved – made the salty journey with us back to dry land. It has the whole of our life at Saltstreet within it. The title – *Some day my prince will come* – is not an irony aimed at me – but at Hesketh herself – her failures – her attempts to protect me – our losses. I understand her so much better now. The day after she'd found us, Fitz went away again – back to her London and her Meredith. There was no reason for her to stay – after all – no need.

Later, I went too – with Hesketh – for a while – but it wasn't as she'd imagined it would be for me – my birthright – too late I suppose. The city – which seemed to Fitz so fertile – was sterile to me. There is so much – or there is nothing – there. Of all the people – wheeling, circling, alighting in their flocks everywhere – there were some I'd heard about always – like Giles – who tried to make us welcome. They took me about everywhere – of course – it was like being ten again – concerts and plays – exhibitions and operas – performance of every variety – artifice in all its forms.

I sometimes saw Fitz – met her warm-hearted mother – even went to her little theatre once. That was the only time I glimpsed what it must be like for them – the audience like a cocktail party out in the cobbled mews with their drinks – then trooping in to sit in the dark room on stools or sofas – where Fitz made it seem not like a garage converted to her workshop – but a world – while Meredith watched her – smiling. I realised they were happy. Hesketh loved all that – but my pain was confused with that of other griefs – by the waters of Babylon we sat down and wept.

Once they took me up a green hill – one of Fitz's beloved places – crowned with a beech wood – to where there was a

212

view down over the whole city and beyond – to the mirror hills across the river valley. The moon and sun both stood in the sky at once – the seesaw pivot of night and day – the city's pale stone – dark smoke – first lights – embellished with curls of both pink and blue cloud. Beautiful it was – no question – a fine sight – like a stage-set, almost life-like – a painted scene which might convince at distance. As they pointed out the landmarks to me – spires, domes, towers, tree-tops – I felt like some maker of sea-charts set to draw an urban map – not utterly lost – but still uncomfortably other. What they saw was not what I saw.

When people told me that the place was weary – war-torn – dishevelled – perhaps permanently spoiled – I answered that to me the ruins seemed noble – the dirt and squalor, which the citizens so much deplored, merely a surface flotsam. Its restoration would only make it more of a mirage to me – the fata morgana glimmering with its deceptive solidity. Buildings – architecture – inland trees – town water – I might have grown used to – but not the multitudes of people – both the crowds I constantly saw and the others whose stories were indefatigably told me – past citizens who still inhabit these old streets. Their immemorial numbers weighed on me like a paving-stone on the heart.

It wasn't my place – I felt foreign – the sea sang in my veins as I sat on the bus – I sniffed the tidal breeze as it ran up the river – my thoughts were all of the beach. When the salt water turned downriver – back to the sea – I felt its tug in my blood – as I felt the surge when it rushed in under the bridges. In the night sometimes I called to mind Crambo – imagined him alone asleep in his sandhills – on his deserted beach. I envied him his cold awakenings under that pearl-inlaid sky – the sea's voice close – the day empty ahead. I pictured him in his solitude again – lord of the foreshore now – a survivor of the burning time and inundation. This thought I took with me – a small potent relic of the beach – the pebble in the pocket drumming its tattoo of home.

I understood how it had been for Fitz – exiled from her own place – not on a holiday or a visit – but with no prospect of home – no return ticket – belonging elsewhere. It was the same for me – that sense of life in the wrong country – I couldn't do, I could only be. After Hesketh had gone I didn't want to stay there – this is the only place I could be without her. *Our revels now are ended.*

I came back to Crambo – prince of the island – who was my childhood sweetheart – if not my first love – after all. He is no more of a monster than Fitz – maybe less. This seems a better solution that being written out altogether – losing even my story.

Crambo

They've gone away again now. I knew they would, and the sea went back to where it belonged too. Where the boathouse used to stand there's just a slew of stones, like any other rubble heap along the beach. The causeway was swept away, the marsh choked with sand-laden mud. It doesn't matter. Everything changes, moves around, comes back again for a while. They rebuilt the seawall, dredged the channel, tried to make a bulwark of concrete blocks across the tide's path to the dunes, but the sea threw them about like cork floats and came licking the dunes' feet anyway. All their rubbish, the wire and bags and mines and dirt, hasn't spoiled the beach, even though it hurts it, the sea is too big. They can't contain it, though they try.

Hesketh took Herself off, left me free to go about my business, disappeared and took Her magic with Her. (Unless She lost that in the sea and had to leave it behind. I don't know. The black dog wasn't in the boat.) Trousers went too, and the soldiers, I outlasted them all. Nobody comes here now, they are all afraid that the sea is poisoned, that the beach will explode beneath their feet, that eating the fish will send them mad. My tainted kingdom, my contaminated realm, is mine again. Except that Kezia came back. She wasn't gone for long.

My island I give to Kezia, all of it from the whale wishbone along along to beyond the concrete box which still smells of soldiers however often the sea swabs it, out to the wreck, in to the church green where she sleeps in the cottage. She prefers that, being inside, but in summer sometimes she stays out on the beach with me. I make her a shrine, and we swim with the seals and dive into the wreck for oyster-shells. Every

215

day I bring her tribute, flowers and stones, things that I find, presents from the tideline, glass and tins and old rope. I think she likes this. And at night sometimes, when the moon is full, I dance to her on the shoreline, on the dune tops, on the pebble ridge or the marsh turf, on my mother's round grave where she lies curled like a fossil waiting for the sea to wake her.

Two Ravens Press is the most remote literary publisher in the UK, operating from a working croft by the sea, right at the end of the most westerly road on the Isle of Lewis in the Outer Hebrides. Our approach to publishing is as radical as our location: Two Ravens Press is run by two writers with a passion for language and for books that are non-formulaic and that take risks. We publish cutting-edge and innovative contemporary fiction, nonfiction and poetry.

Visit our website for comprehensive information on all of our books and authors – and for much more:

- browse all Two Ravens Press books (print books and e-books too) by category or by author, and purchase them online at an average 20% discount on retail price, post & packing-free (in the UK, and for a small fee overseas)

- there is a separate page for each book, including summaries, extracts and reviews, and one for each of our authors, including interviews, biographies and photographs

- you can also find us on Facebook: become a fan of the Two Ravens Press page, and automatically receive all our news and updates about new books.

www.tworavenspress.com